BATTLETECH:
ELEMENTS OF TREASON: OPPORTUNITY

BY CRAIG A. REED, JR.

BATTLETECH: ELEMENTS OF TREASON: OPPORTUNITY
By Craig A. Reed, Jr.
Cover art and design by Tan Ho Sim
Interior art by Alan Blackwell, Aaron Harris, Duane Loose, Justin Nelson, Matt Plog,
    Anthony Scroggins, Franz Vohwinkel, David White

Printed in USA.

Published by Catalyst Game Labs,
an imprint of InMediaRes Productions, LLC
5003 Main St. #110 • Tacoma, WA 98407

CHAPTER 1

MONOLITH-CLASS JUMPSHIP *EVENING STAR*
CHAPULTEPEC NADIR POINT
JADE FALCON OCCUPATION ZONE
22 JANUARY 3151

Duke Vedet Brewer nodded. "Are you sure?"

The words hung in the air for several seconds, the people floating around the holotable unwilling to commit to an answer. Finally, the *Evening Star*'s captain, a pale, stocky man whose usually drooping mustache was floating above his lip like a wild animal, nodded. "Aye, Your Grace. We can't find a trace of any Falcon forces in the system."

Vedet looked around the table. He was a rangy man with walnut-colored skin and an unremarkable face. Despite being past sixty, his short hair-and-circle beard—a mustache/goatee combination—was still as dark as it had been twenty years ago. "Anyone think it might be a trap?"

Kommandant-Hauptmann Helen Goreson, CO of the Hesperus Guards' First Battalion, shook her head. She was slightly below medium height, thick without being fat, with blondish hair cut close to her scalp. "Ain't the Birdies style," she said in a nasal drawl, the scars on her face standing out against her paling skin.

"Agreed," Colonel Thomas Kirk, the Guards' field commander, added.

Brewer looked around the holotable. The senior officers of his own Hesperus Guards and the *Evening Star*'s captain returned his stare. *I once commanded hundreds of billions*, he thought ruefully. *Now, I command only a couple of thousand.*

He had once been the Archon of the Lyran Commonwealth, a ruler of over three hundred star systems. Now, he wasn't quite a fugitive, but he wasn't welcome in many parts of the Commonwealth. The fact he wasn't being hunted by the Lyran Commonwealth Armed Forces or the Lyran Intelligence Corps showed the weakness of Archon Trillian Steiner and the Commonwealth itself. The Commonwealth was in freefall, a stumbling, weakened state that had lost dozen of worlds to both the Wolf and Jade Falcon Clans, ripe to be ripped apart by enemies on all its borders.

Melissa, you fool!

After years of dithering, Melissa Steiner, the Archon before him, had let her ambition run ahead of her ability by trying to stabilize the Commonwealth at the expense of both the former Free Worlds League and the Republic of the Sphere. She then doubled down by allowing the Wolves to freely move through the Commonwealth to help the LCAF in its war against former Free Worlds planets. When the Wolves had turned on Melissa, seized a dozen Lyran worlds and mauled the LCAF, their betrayal had sent shockwaves through the state. A cabal of LCAF generals decided they weren't going to be held responsible for the Archon's mistakes. They staged a coup, removed Melissa, and allowing Brewer to step in and try to save the Commonwealth.

But the job had proved impossible, and when both the Wolves and Falcons came for Tharkad, he and his Hesperus Guards had fled, repudiated by the same generals who had put him into power, leaving Melissa back on the throne and to a martyr's death. Now, Melissa's shadow, her cousin Trillian, was the Archon and was proving to be just as ineffective as her deceased cousin.

"Any activity from the planet itself?" he asked.

"Nothing yet," Brewer's head of intelligence replied. Midori Jennings was tall, gaunt, and pale. With a high forehead, thin face, and blank expression, more than a few of the Hesperus Guards called him "The Undertaker" behind his back, but Brewer found him to be capable and competent. "My people are already monitoring for any signals from the planet. We should have a better idea in a day or two."

Vedet nodded. "Good."

The flight from Tharkad to Alekseyevka had given him a better idea of the Commonwealth's condition—and it wasn't good. Discontent was everywhere—on the news, on talk shows, in anti-Archon demonstrations on planet after planet. His own actions hadn't been spared from the anger, and something inside of him agreed with their belief.

He and the surviving Hesperus Guards had landed on Alekseyevka. He had tried to set up a government in exile there, still claiming to be Archon. But that had died a quick death, leaving him with nowhere to go.

Bitter and angry, he had taken a hard look at himself and saw an arrogant and foolish man who had done everything wrong and paid the price. No, if he wanted power, he was going to have to take a different path. And that meant learning.

"What about sending a recon force to the planet?" Goreson asked. She had been with the Guards from the start, rising from lance command to the First's 'Mech Battalion's CO on ability alone.

Vedet looked at the *Evening Star*'s captain. "Hank?"

Captain Hank Volman returned his Duke's stare. "It'll be a fifteen-day round trip from Chapultepec and back."

Vedet shook his head. "Too much time. We'll finish our recharge and jump to Melissia like we planned." He shifted his attention to Jennings. "If you came up with anything you think I should know about, contact me."

"Yes, Your Grace."

The duke looked around the table. "It looks like the Birds are going to ignore us, but we do not know if that's a good or bad thing. Stay at Condition Two and be ready for anything. That is all, ladies and gentlemen."

As his staff moved away, Vedet let his feet touch the deck and felt his boot's magnetic soles take hold. Taking a deep breath, he tapped a few buttons on the holotable's control panel and a map of the surrounding solar systems appeared. He stared at it for a few moments, familiarizing himself where the systems were in relation to each other before tapping a few buttons. One system enlarged to take up the entire table space. He stared at it silently.

"Your Grace?"

Vedet glanced at Jennings, who was standing there, his own magnetic boots holding him in place. "Yes?"

"May I ask why you are staring so intently at the Melissia system?"

"It's our final destination. I'm familiarizing myself with the system."

Jennings tilted his head slightly. "You had repeated familiarizing yourself with the system five times in the last forty-eight hours."

Vedet smiled slightly. "You keeping count?"

"Not really, Your Grace. But you seem..." The spymaster thought for a moment. "... intense regarding Melissia."

"Why not? It was a district capital before the Clanners took it. The perfect place to establish ourselves."

"If you don't mind me saying, I have not seen you act so—"

"—obsessive?" Vedet said, then chuckled. "I'm not. But I spent several months on Melissia when I was a young man." He sighed. "Some of the best days of my life."

"I see, Your Grace," Jennings said in a tone that stated he didn't.

"Maybe one day I'll tell you. But for now, please leave me."

The spymaster bowed and disengaged his boots' magmatic soles before floating away from the holotable.

Vedet watched him leave, then his eyes went back to the displayed system.

I should have never left you, Cassandra, he thought.

CHAPTER 2

Graf Yiorgos Laskaris stared through his binoculars at the battle below. His command group, guarded by a battalion of his Fylakes and a mercenary 'Mech company, were on a cliff top, while the battle went on below. The Melissian Republic forces were dug in around the town of Banskon, which straddled the Broad Run River and one of the major routes into Republic-held territory.

The Noble Council forces, roughly four mixed regiments of infantry, armor, and 'Mechs, were heavily engaged with the Republic forces, several regiments backed up by some armor and a few BattleMechs. Smoke drifted over the battlefield, hiding some of the fighting from Laskaris' view.

He lowered his binoculars. He was above middle height, with short blond hair, light brown skin, blue eyes, and a round face. "Colonel Maldonado!"

Colonel Tricia Maldonado, the council's senior mercenary commander, who was standing a couple of meters away, looked over at the Graf. She was a tall, thin woman with a blue-green Mohawk and a scarred face. "Yes, Your Grace?"

"Order Palcott's lance to move upriver and ford the river like we planned. Move Trimes' lance up to Palcott's position and have them ready to move up when I give the word."

"Yes, Your Grace."

Yiorgos smiled, half-listening to Maldonado relaying his orders, and returned to watching the battle below. The Republicans were stubborn, he would give them that. But they hung onto positions too long, unwilling to give up land to the Council's forces. Once Palcott's lance was over the river, they could strike the defenses on the other side of the river, maybe even kill the enemy commander.

"Your Grace," Maldonado said. "Baron Gettle is requesting reinforcements and BattleMechs."

The graf shifted his attention to the right, where Baron Gettle's forces were trying to force their way into an industrial zone south of the city's center. "What forces do we have to support him?"

"We have two light 'Mech lances that can reach the baron in three minutes, and a medium lance in four minutes."

"Send the medium lance and that platoon of Manticores. The lights may be faster, but the mediums have more firepower and armor." *Plus*, he thought, *that extra minute will bleed the good baron's forces a bit more.*

"Yes, your grace."

Yiorgos's smile widened into a full grin as he lowered his binoculars again and turned toward his own 'Mech, a pristine *Titan II*. "Come on, Colonel," he said to Maldonado as he walked past her. "I want to shift locations."

"Yes, Your Grace."

Callisto Mylonasa ducked as another shell slammed into the building about the underground headquarters. The lightstrips flickered, and Callisto felt herself covered in fine particles of matter from the ceiling above. Behind her, Republic Vice-Minister Andrea Tippet ignored the dust and ferrocrete fragments that cascaded down on them.

They were similar in some ways and very different in others. Both women were tall and lean, but Callisto had long dark hair done up in a braid, jade-green eyes, and mahogany skin. Tippet had a pinched face, a long neck, short graying hair, and slightly tanned skin. Both wore field uniforms, body armor and helmets, though Tippet's were less worn and cleaner than Callisto's.

They strode down the narrow hallway, Callisto with wariness, Tippet with arrogant indifference. Several times, Republican soldiers, wearing the same sort of uniforms, rushed past them, forcing the two the step aside as soldiers came at them. Callisto heard Tippet sniff as a wide-eyes private ran past them at a full sprint. "No discipline," she said.

Callisto lightly bit her tongue to prevent herself from turning around and telling the vice-minister she was wrong. But Tippet had the ear of her Freedom Party leaders, while Callisto had a post as an advisor to the Prime Minister, who was in power only at the sufferance of those same party leaders. Combined with Callisto's half-brother leading the Noble Council, her position was tenuous, at best.

As they reached the entrance to the command post, another round slammed into the building above them, releasing another shower of dust.

Inside, it was mayhem. A half-dozen soldiers were moving from one place to another, shouting out reports toward a central table, where a trio of officers stood, tapping buttons on the flat-screen table.

Tippet shouldered her way past Callisto. "Colonel Nathanson," she said in an imperious tone. "What is the situation?"

One man at the table, a younger man wearing the three stars of a Melissian Republic Colonel, looked up at both women. He was shorter than Tippet, but broader, with short platinum-blond hair and a face most would call solid. "The situation?" Mason Nathanson replied. "The situation is drastic and getting worse."

"How can it be drastic?" Tippet's tone was clipped and biting at the same time. "We must hold Banskon."

"Well, The Council wants it badly."

"Our soldiers will hold, if given the right leadership."

"Really?" Mason fired back. "We're outnumbered four to one in 'Mechs, three to one in armor and five to one in infantry. Plus, Yiorgos himself is commanding the attack—he may be a slimy bastard, but he's competent." Another round landed somewhere above them, filling the air with dust. "Did I mention we're also getting hammered with artillery?"

Tippet folded her arms. "You will defend Banskon. To the last man, if you must."

Mason shook his head, and Callisto could see the anger in his eyes. "I will do no such thing. Your position as Vice Minister of Diplomatic Affairs does not place you in my chain of command, and thus you have no authority over me. Also, the Prime Minister has made it clear to all field commanders that last-stands will not be tolerated or ordered, not after Makrychori."

"They will remember Ajax Kostoulas as a Hero of the Republic."

Mason's tone was hard as steel and he didn't bother hiding his anger. "Kostoulas was a fool, and his stupidity needlessly caused his death and that of five thousand of his soldiers."

Tippet stiffened. "How dare—"

"I dare to speak the *truth*, Vice Minister," Mason growled. Callisto noticed the rest of the command post had gone silent, everyone looking at the confrontation in the center of the room. "From the start, Makrychori was not only militarily insignificant, but impossible to hold with ten thousand soldiers. They ordered Kostoulas to pull back to a better defensive position, but he refused to do so. He disobeyed his orders, and the Republic lost five thousand soldiers in a needless defensive action!" He turned back to the table, dismissing Tippet from his attentions.

Callisto couldn't see Tippet's face, but the vice minister's body was trembling in rage. "Colonel Nathanson!" she snarled. "You are—"

"Colonel!" a tech yelled. "We have enemy 'Mechs to the north of the city, on the east side of the river!"

Mason tapped a few keys and stared at the screen that was the top of the table. "Do we have any reserves left?"

"Just your command lance!"

"Damn." Mason muttered. "That's it," he unfastened his uniform top, showing the cooling vest he wore underneath. "Comms, put out the word. Retreat Plan Delta. Barlow?"

A thin woman with frizzy hair looked up from her console. "Yes, sir?"

"How long to take this all down and get it loaded up?"

"Fifteen minutes."

"You have ten." Mason turned to look at Tippet. "You better get going." he looked at Callisto. "Both of you."

"You're giving up?" Tippet growled.

"No, I'm falling back before we're surrounded and cut off. Mylonas, escort our guests to the command vehicle and make sure they're strapped in."

"Colonel!" Callisto said quickly. "I need to speak to you for a moment!"

Mason stared at her for a couple of seconds then nodded. "Fine, we can speak on the way to my 'Mech. Come on."

Callisto had to hurry after the colonel, who rapidly walked out of the room. Instead of turning right, the way she and Tippet had come from, Mason turned left and headed down the narrow hallway, Callisto right behind him. A right turn at the end of the hallway took them to a set of rough wooden stairs leading up.

Instead of climbing the stairs, Mason turned and pulled Callisto under them. "You shouldn't have come," he said, looking up at her. Callisto was half a head taller than him, but it didn't matter to her.

"I had to," she replied in a fierce whisper before kissing him.

He didn't resist her kisses—he never did—but after a few seconds, he pushed her away. "This is the worst place to be!"

"I don't care!" Callisto replied. "I came to warn you that the Freedom Party is setting you up to take the blame for this. They set you up."

He nodded. "Thought as much. Tippet the hatchet woman?"

"Yes, I think she was about to relieve you of duty when the 'Mech report came in."

"Thank god for small favors. Not that any of my officers would have obeyed her. Don't worry. I have enough ammo of my own to counter them."

"The PM said he supports any decision you make."

"Good to know someone else is in my corner."

They kissed again, Mason taking the lead this time before he broke it again. "Get to the command vehicle. I'll hold off the incoming 'Mechs."

"Won't Yiorgos realize who you are when he see your 'Mech?"

"Don't worry. That one is still back at the Rock. I'm using a *Linebacker* we cobbled together for my current machine." He touched his finger to her lip. "When the time comes, I'll face Yiorgos in my uncle's 'Mech." He guided her out from under the stairs. "Get going. I'll see you back at the Rock."

Callisto nodded and hurried away. "Please, god, keep him safe," she muttered as she ran down the hall.

She didn't look back.

CHAPTER 3

After a small dinner—he had eaten the same meals as the crew to make sure everything was as it should be—Vedet retreated to his cabin and continued reading a book on military history, one of hundreds he had brought along. He sat on his bunk, the noteputer on one thigh, and a pad of paper on the other for notes.

On Alekseyevka, he had decided on a course of self-education. He began reading, attending classes at a local university, and having public debates with local leaders. He had thought himself to be a political animal, but quickly realized he was out of his depth and hadn't even known it. While he was already well-versed in business and economics, he dove deep into both of these new subjects, expanding his knowledge in both areas.

But it wasn't just the civilian side of things, either. As he read more military history, Vedet realized his own victories had been due more to good fortune and the soldiers under his command. He dove deeper into military subjects with the same determination he had with the civilian subjects. Tactics, strategy, logistics, anything that would give him a better understanding of what he had done wrong.

Once he had thrown himself into learning what he had done wrong, he realized he needed people with skills he didn't have. Midori Jennings had been a member of LIC before being rendered "redundant" in one of former Archon Melissa's shakeups. After several long conversations, he'd hired Jennings to run his intelligence arm.

In 3146, Jennings' first test was to gather intelligence on the newly formed Buena Collective and its new leader, Diego Widmer. The former LCAF general and Margrave of Timbuktu had offered Vedet and his forces sanctuary in the Collective. Vedet was considering the offer, but needed to make an informed decision.

It had taken three months for the new head of intelligence to put together a team and set up a network, and another three months for the data to come in. It was another two months before Jennings briefed the Duke on the results.

"In short," Jennings had said, "the Collective is too weak to stand on its own for any major length of time. I predict it will not last more than five years if left on its own, less if the Commonwealth sends a military force."

"And if we get involved?" Vedet had asked.

"Committing the First Hesperus to defense of the Collective will add only six months to their lifespan, and will cause the First to take medium to heavy losses."

Vedet had done his own investigating, spoke to experts, read, and used his new knowledge to try to poke holes in Jennings' reports. In the meantime, he stalled Widmer's offers to become part of the Collective's military, citing a lack of parts and training. While the offers were easily diverted, finding holes in Jennings' assessment was much harder.

After careful consideration and to give Jennings a better look at the conditions in the Collective, Vedet had moved the First to Rapla, two jumps from Buena, Widmer's capital. While not actually taking up Widmer's offer, the gesture was enough to placate the warlord—for now.

The next six months were a show. Vedet continued his education, while the First trained as if they were short of parts and personnel. Jennings had assured Vedet that Widmer had spies on-planet, and Vedet had made it look like the First was worse off than they actually were.

Meanwhile, Jennings sharpened his assessment, and it was worse than the original. Trillian Steiner had been silent on the Collective beyond refusing to recognize it. But Jennings predicted the LCAF would send a force to retake Buena and the other Collective worlds, and it would happen within three years.

After meeting with the First Hesperus' command staff, Vedet decided it would be better to stay on Rapla. He made a show of increasing the training, recruitment and buying of supplies. His niece, Caroline Brewer, Hesperus II's regent, sent several shipments of spare parts, 'Mechs, vehicles, and battle armor to Rapla to fill out the units. Jennings continued his intelligence gathering, and Vedet continued his learning.

In 3148, when the Commonwealth sent a military force into the Collective—six months later than Jennings predicted— Vedet's decision to stay out of the conflict was an easy one. Jennings' analysis of the situation had sharpened to where he believed Widmer was going to lose and lose badly. Vedet's own feeling was that the Collective was doomed, and he wouldn't waste his First Hesperus Guards for a losing side. So he and the First had stayed on Rapla. When Widmer had sent one last plea, Vedet's reply was simple and to the point: *I hope you have an exit strategy.*

But while he would not get involved with the Collective, he realized the longer he and the First stayed outside of Archon Trillian Steiner's control, the more of a threat he would become to those in power. So he had reached out to old contracts, including Gareth Dinesen, one of the generals in the cabal that had put Brewer on the Archon's throne. Relations between the two were cool—Dinesen and his cabal had been just as quick to abandon him when the Jade Falcons and Wolves had come for Tharkad.

Dinesen had agreed to talk to Vedet, but only face-to-face. The margrave was on Adelaide, one jump from the Jade Falcon border. About the same time, the breakaway Timbuktu Collective along the Periphery began moving to claim more Commonwealth worlds and Archon Trillian had requested that Vedet and the Hesperus Guards intervene.

So Vedet and the Hesperus Guards began a series of jumps—not toward the Collective, but to the Falcon border instead. On Adelaide, Dinesen had finally agreed to back Brewer again with both money and influence. In return for the support, Dinesen wanted Melissia back from the Falcons—his Melissia theater was a victim of the Falcons' rampage—and he had no forces to retake the planets he'd lost. He was willing to back Vedet and his people to do it, seeing it as a way to show how weak Archon Trillian Steiner was.

Dinesen had thought Vedet Brewer was going to liberate Melissia to make Trillian look weak and reestablish Brewer's claim to be Archon. But Vedet had his own plans, ones he kept to himself. Melissia was a theater capital, surrounded by planets controlled by the Jade Falcons, with enough infrastructure to make a perfect place to put his plans in motion.

In short, a perfect place to start a new empire.

There was a knock on the cabin hatch. "Enter," Vedet called out.

The hatch slid open and Jennings stepped into the cabin. "Your Grace."

Vedet looked at the chronograph on the bulkhead. "You're up late."

The hatch slid closed behind Jennings. "As are you, Your Grace."

Brewer waved a hand. "The demands of leadership."

"Yes, Your Grace."

"What brings you here?"

Jennings stepped over to the bunk and held out a noteputer to the duke. "Communications from the planet, Your Grace."

Vedet took the noteputer and started scanning the text. The longer he read, the less sense it made to him. "It sounds like the Falcons...have pulled out?"

"It appears so."

Brewer looked up at him. "Could this be some sort of trap?"

"Doubtful. It took time for those signals to reach us, and we have not been here long enough for the signals to be sent after we arrived. And three different people currently claiming to be Chapultepec's leader? Assuming this is some sort of trap, it is unlike the Falcons. Malvina is as subtle as an avalanche."

"And just as deadly."

"But it does lend some validity to the rumors that the Falcons have abandoned their holdings and made a drive for Terra."

Vedet snorted. "It's just that, rumors. There's still that wall around Terra, remember? Or do you think Malvina figured out how to get past it?"

"It would be more likely that Alaric has discovered a way to penetrate the fortress."

The Duke's face darkened in anger, then he nodded. "Maybe." He sighed. "I've been out of the loop for too long, Midori."

Wolf Khan Alaric Ward was the main reason Brewer had replaced Melissa Steiner as Archon, and then lost the throne less than two years later. When he had first met the Khan during the Lyran campaign against the Free Worlds League, Brewer found him to be impossibly arrogant, with an ego the size of a planet. Only after grudgingly fighting alongside him in the battle against Anson Marik and the Silver Hawk Irregulars on Stewart in 3138 did Brewer see the true warrior behind the ego.

Alaric was the worst kind of opponent—one with the vision to rule and the skills to back it up. While that revelation had soothed Vedet's ego somewhat, it left him feeling disappointed in himself for being outmaneuvered by a man more than twenty years younger than him.

"Yes, Your Grace," Jenning replied. "Anything else?"

Vedet handed the noteputer to Jennings. "As of right now, my orders stand. Continue recharging and preparing to jump to Melissia. Also, see what you can work up on an enemy force on Melissia, assuming they pull all the garrisons in the sector back to there. Best and worst cases."

Jennings took the noteputer. "Yes, Your Grace."

"Then get some sleep. If the Falcons have pulled their garrisons back to Melissia, we could be in the fight of our lives."

"Yes, Your Grace. You should follow your own advice. If there is a fight coming, we will need your leadership."

"Don't worry about me. I'll be ready when the times comes."

CHAPTER 4

MONOLITH-CLASS JUMPSHIP *EVENING STAR*
CHAPULTEPEC NADIR POINT
JADE FALCON OCCUPATION ZONE
29 JANUARY 3151

Brewer's command staff assembled again, though there was an air of confusion and uncertainty among them. Internally, Brewer smiled. He didn't want his staff to become complacent.

"Right," he said, leaning on the holotable. "I take it you have all heard the message our intelligence people picked up?"

There were nods and muttered agreements around the holotable. Brewer waited until they had quieted down again. "I want your opinions and your questions."

"How did we get the signal?" asked Colonel Clarence Peterson, commander of the Guards' infantry. He was a large, bony man with rough features and a gravelly voice.

Kirk replied, "We picked up the following signal just after we jumped in, and one of our commtechs passed her free time while we were recharging trying to decrypt it. When she did so a few hours ago, she immediately informed her superior, and it was quickly sent up to Midori."

"I've read the transcript," Brewer said. "Opinions?"

"It sounds like the Falcon garrison has departed Chapultepec and headed off to God knows where," Kirk replied. "And it looks like the planet's population has staged a rebellion."

"That is consistent with all the other data we have collected from the planet so far," Jennings said. "We're picking up only commercial traffic, and almost nothing on military channels, clear or encrypted."

Colonel Denise Wilson, commander of the Guards' armor brigades, rubbed her chin. "Sounds awfully convenient, if you ask me."

"Could it be bait to lure us into an ambush?" Peterson asked.

Goreson shook her head. "Way outside the Budgies' normal operating procedures."

"Agreed," Brewer replied. "Care to add anything else, Thomas?"

Kirk nodded. "Our best estimate of the signal is that they sent it several hours before we even arrived in-system. To do something like that, they would have to have known we were coming."

"Which is very unlikely." Brewer looked around the table. "I know we were supposed to jump in two hours, but I'm delaying that for the moment."

"Why?" Captain Volman asked.

Brewer tapped a few keys on the holotable control panel and the image of a planetary system appeared. "Ladies and gentlemen, the Melissia system."

He let them stare at the system's image for a few seconds before adjusting a knob on the control panel. The image zoomed in onto a single planet and its moon. "This is Melissia V and its moon, Saratoga. Instead of our original plan of jumping in at the L-One point and heading full-bore for the planet—" Brewer expanded the view to encompass the entire Melissia system, "—I propose we use the L-One point for Melissia III instead, which is still well within range to monitor communications, and will minimize Melissia V's knowledge of our presence—they'll detect that we've entered the system, but nothing more than that. Then we give Jennings' people seventy-two hours to see what they can gather from the planet's transmissions. I want to find out if the Falcons are there, and if so, in what strength. Once we know what's going on, then we can decide how to proceed. Any comment?"

Volmer looked at the holotable image. "Standard Lagrange point. Should be easy to recalculate the jump."

"I think we should have the aerospace boys and girls standing by," Goreson said. "Just in case."

"Agreed. I want all aerospace fighters on standby when we jump in, but no one launches without my direct order. If there are no surprises waiting for us, I want half the aerospace force on five-minute alert, the other half off, rotating every six hours."

He changed his gaze to Volman, who also functioned as the commander of the Guards' space transport assets. "I want the same sort of thing with the DropShips' gunners—fully manned when we jump in, then fifty percent manned, fifty percent off, every six hours." He looked around the table. "We could be looking at either a ripe plum waiting to drop into our hand, or a poisoned fruit. Let's not assume either until we know more facts."

CHAPTER 5

OVERLORD-CLASS DROPSHIP *HESPERUS ONE*
MELISSIA SYSTEM
JADE FALCON OCCUPATION ZONE
2 FEBRUARY 3151

"May I have this dance?"

The woman, nearly as tall as Vedet, dark hair that flowed down her back. Her skin was flawless, the color of mahogany, and her face was the equal of any goddess'. Lively green eyes, the color of grass, gazed at him, taking in the sight. Her light-blue dress was the height of fashion, both modest and revealing, showing a well-toned body and fluidity of motion.

When he smiled, he felt a jolt of pleasure go through him. "Why not?' she said, her voice warm and sweet. "Would you like to lead, or shall I?"

Someone knocking on his hatch brought Vedet out of his pleasant dream. "Who is it?"

"Jennings, Your Grace. I have the latest data compilation."

"Enter."

Jennings walked in as he sat up. "Forgive the earliness of the hour."

Brewer sat and saw it was early. He sighed and ran his fingers across his hair. "Don't apologize. I was the one who ordered the data be given to me as soon as it was ready. What do we have?"

The jump had been successful, and for the past sixty-five hours, the Guards' SIGINT section, aided by Jennings' small team of analysts, had been monitoring all broadcasts from Melissia V and been evaluating the signals.

Jennings handed Brewer a noteputer. "It is as we suspected. The Fifth Falcon Talon Cluster is no longer on-planet. They left a small *solahma* and paramilitary force behind. The local population seized the opportunity to overwhelm the garrison and seized control of the Rock and the capital of Europa. They've declared an independent government—the Melissian Republic—and currently control about sixty percent of the planetary landmass."

"Who controls the other forty percent?"

"A collection of nobles. When the Falcons took over the planet, they isolated and cut off sections of the planetary population they deemed useless to their war effort. These areas were left to fend for themselves, and it came down to the local nobles taking command and leading the people to survive. When the Republic tried to extend into those areas, they met armed resistance from the local population—suspiciously armed resistance, considering how isolated they had been. The Noble Council drove the Republic out of Europa and back to the Rock. Now, there is a standoff between the two sides, with an active battle front."

Vedet glanced through the data. "Force strength?"

"The Republic has about fifteen infantry regiments, two regiments of armor and a battalion of BattleMechs, all salvage, mercenary, or leftover from the Falcon garrison. The Nobles can field about six brigades of mixed infantry, three of armor and a near regiment of BattleMechs, mostly older Inner Sphere models. Right now, the Nobles are involved in a sustained offense in the Broad Run River Valley and have most of the valley under their control. Bandits are operating across the continent of Jahreszeitwunder, especially near the mountains to the north."

Vedet took several minutes to read the summary from the noteputer, then handed back to Jennings. "Inform the command staff there will be an officer's meeting at 0900 hours, and make sure they all get that summary. I want Foster and Leeson there too."

"Yes, Your Grace."

After Jennings left, Vedet didn't go back to bed. Instead, he got out of his bunk and floated over to a small case that was part of his luggage. He opened it and looked through the case, careful not to send things floating out of the case. After a moment, he found what he was looking for. A necklace with a ring hanging from it.

He gazed at the ring on the thin silver necklace. The necklace was dull with age, but the ring was as perfect as it had been all those years ago when he had brought it. The diamond was the size of his fingernail on his little finger, surrounded by slivers of ruby and emeralds, all set into a golden band. Even after all this time, the sight of it took his breath away.

He didn't know how long he stared at it, but after a while, he looped the necklace over his head until he settled onto his chest. He hadn't worn it in years, but it felt right there, over his heart. He closed the case, floated back to his bunk, and climbed in.

Cassie, he thought before he closed his eyes and allowed himself to be drawn into that dance with the dark-haired woman with the green eyes.

CHAPTER 6

MONOLITH-CLASS JUMPSHIP *EVENING STAR*
MELISSIA SYSTEM
JADE FALCON OCCUPATION ZONE
FEBRUARY 2 3151

By the time Brewer floated into the JumpShip's conference room, the rest of his command staff had already arrived and talking among themselves. The conversations died as he approached the holotable. "Good morning," he said, looking around the table, looking each man and woman in the eye before moving on. "I take it you have all read the summary SIGINT has compiled?"

There was a murmur of *"yes"* and more than a few nods from the assembled staff.

Brewer nodded. "What is your opinion of the situation on the planet?"

"Damn near perfect for us," Goreson said. "They don't seem to know we're here, and they're too busy trying to kill each other to realize it."

"Agreed," Kirk said. "We could launch decapitation strikes at both capitals at the same time. Europa isn't a problem, but we're going to need time to come up with a plan to hit the Rock."

"We can control the air with no problems," said Kommandant Janelle LeSat, the aerospace commander.

Peterson shook his head. "We'd be heavily outnumbered once we're on the ground. If the two sides decide we're the bigger enemy, it could get messy quickly. They would swamp my infantry with sheer numbers."

"Our 'Mechs are better," Goreson replied.

The infantry commander shook his head. "Maybe, but they can only shoot at so many targets at a time. They have numbers and knowledge of the land. They could lose a dozen battles and still overwhelm us."

"That's why we go with the decapitation strikes," Kirk said. "Take out the leaders, and the military will be rudderless."

Brewer nodded. "Yes, we could launch decapitation strikes." He paused. "But we won't."

The puzzled looks from his staff made him smile. "Colonel Peterson is right; we are outnumbered, and fighting will cost both sides necessary soldiers and materiel. We've all seen what happens when a planet is occupied. So, I propose we go in not as occupiers, but as allies and liberators. So, instead of storming our way through the front door, we're going to knock and ask politely to come in."

He looked at the two people who had been standing in the corner. "You all know Hiram Foster and Zabrina Leeson."

The pair were a contrast in almost everything. Foster was a tall, lean man, with short brown hair going gray, a patrician face, and dressed in a casually elegant way. Leeson was a shorter, stockier woman, with a broader face and long blond hair collected into a short braid.

"These two will be my envoys," Brewer continued, returning his gaze to his command staff. "Foster will speak to the nobles and Leeson will speak to the Melissian Republic. They will carry a personal video message from me, expressing my interest in helping them. Clarence, I want two squads of your best soldiers, full dress uniforms and parade-level shine and discipline, one squad to go with each envoy. Janelle, I want a pair of your aerospace fighters, parade-ready and tight formation, to escort each shuttle down to the planet and return here afterward. It won't hurt to show some teeth in our smile."

"Your Grace," Jennings said. "In the last couple of hours, we've determined that Melissia's planetary space tracking system was one casualty in the uprising and subsequent fighting. They cannot track anything outside of the atmosphere."

Brewer turned and smiled at this news. "Really? How many spy satellites do we have onboard?"

"Six, Your Grace."

"Deploy four of them to cover the main front between the two sides." He turned back to Foster and Leeson. "You two will act as if the other envoy doesn't exist. Let them think I'm dealing with only one side—they might be a little more forthcoming that way. Get to know both each sides' main players and what they want. Also, assess their political, economic, and military structure. Communicate using Gamma encryption."

"Yes, Your Grace," the two said.

"Now," Brewer said, looking back at his commanders. "Any other questions?"

CHAPTER 7

The mood in the conference room was a hostile one. Callisto felt it as soon as she walked in, following Prime Minister Nicholas Mendez. If Mendez felt it, he said nothing as he walked to the head of the conference table. Callisto nodded to Mason Nathanson, who was standing behind the Defense Minister's chair, and followed Mendez.

There were twelve people seated at the table, the Melissian Republic's senior leadership. The prime minister sat, while Callisto took up a spot behind his chair. Mendez was a stout man with a face that had seen its share of violence, graying hair, and stone-gray eyes.

"Citizens," he said in a rough voice. "I take it you have all heard the news?"

Tippet sniffed loudly. "It's some sort of trick."

Mendez looked at her. "Is it?"

Tippet sniffed again. "I agree with Minister McCarron in that—"

"How is the minister?" Mendez asked.

His question stopped her in mid-sentence. "Still weak," she replied after a few seconds.

"Please convey my best wishes for his speedy recovery."

Tippet nodded sharply. "I will do so. But it doesn't change the fact that both the minister and I agree this envoy is some sort of trap."

"And you came to that conclusion without speaking to them?" Defense Minister Dennis Marsch asked. He was a medium-built man with a hook nose and deep-set eyes. "Your powers of observation are astounding."

Tippet shot him a scowl. "I would not be speaking so cavalierly, Dennis."

"Duke Brewer is a powerful noble. I wouldn't dismiss a chance to talk to him out of hand."

"He is a *noble*," Tippet growled.

Marsch leaned back in his chair and folded his arms. "So, you're willing to dismiss help because the man behind the offer is nobility?"

"If your soldiers were better led, we would not be in this position!"

The defense minister raised an eyebrow. "Vice-Minister, I am not the one who has been placing 'political reliability' above competence when selecting commanders."

Tippet glared at him, then looked at Nathanson. "Your own selection to command didn't do so well."

"At least Colonel Nathanson retreated with most of his force intact," Marsch replied coolly. "It doesn't do any good to throw away lives for no reason."

"Are you saying our troops are lacking fighting spirit?"

"What they are lacking is competent leadership."

"Enough," Mendez said firmly. "Fighting between ourselves will only benefit Graf Laskaris and his people. It won't hurt us to listen." He turned toward Callisto. "Contact the Duke's representative and inform them we will speak to them."

"Prime Minister!" Tippet exclaimed, rising out of her seat. "You cannot be serious—"

"Vice minister," Mendez said in the same tone. "My decision is final."

Tippet sank into her seat. "As Vice Minister for Diplomatic Affairs, I demand I be involved with the meeting."

Mendez exhaled slowly. "I cannot bar you from the meeting. In fact, I designate you as our lead representative for it, but Miss Mylonasa and Colonel Nathanson will also be there."

"There is no need for that," Tippet said stiffly.

"I think there is a need for both of them."

The vice minister bristled. "I don't trust Mylonasa or Nathanson."

"I trust Mylonasa, and Marsch trusts Nathanson. They will be there to look out for the Republic's interests, just like you."

Tippet leaned forward, his eyes dark and hard. "Remember, Nicholas," she said in a low, hard voice. "You are only in office on our sufferance."

"Remember, Andrea," Mendez replied coolly. "I am in office because the other parties don't trust your Freedom Party with full control of the government."

Tippet's expression didn't change, but she sat back and folded her arms. "For now. But if the Nobles' Council gain control of the Loveless Valley, all bets are off."

"If the Nobles gain control of the Loveless Valley, it won't matter who's the prime minister."

There was silence in the room, stretching for a few seconds to over ten before Tippet looked at Marsch. "If you don't stop the Council forces from entering the Loveless Valley, I want your resignation."

"It's as much as your fault as it's mine for our difficulties," the defense minister replied. "Your fault for installing idiot commanders, and mine for letting you do it."

"Our commanders hold their ground!"

"Until they're wiped out by the Council. I ordered Kostoulas to retreat, to fall back to a better defensive position. But he refused and was wiped out, thinning out our lines and weakening us."

"Ajax Kostoulas died as any Republic soldier should."

"Did any of his soldiers agree with him?"

"Enough," Mendez said. "Kostoulas was an idiot and cost us soldiers and materiel, but he is dead, and I loathe speaking ill of the dead. Andrea, meet with the Duke's representative and found out what he's offering. Questions?" No one said anything. "Fine. Let's move onto the next item on the agenda."

CHAPTER 8

EUROPA
JAHRESZEITWUNDER
MELISSIA
JADE FALCON OCCUPATION ZONE
3 FEBRUARY, 3151

"I don't like this."

Yiorgos Laskaris smiled and shrugged. "Iago, you worry too much."

Baron Iago Pocasio stood in front of Yiorgos' desk and glared at the Graf. "Brewer is a wild card! We don't even know why he's here!"

Yiorgos shook his head and gave Pocasio a sympatric look. "Let's wait and see what his envoy has to say."

Pocasio was the type of man who could blend into the background with ease when he chose to. He was slightly below middle height and on the thin side, with forgettable features. Laskaris had known the man for years, yet the baron was still very much an enigma to him and everyone who knew him. He had proven to be trustworthy, but there was an aloof air about him that left many people on the Noble Council uneasy.

The office was on the top floor of the former Melissia Theater Administration building, now the Noble Council's headquarters. It was the largest and best furnished office in the building, and used whenever Yiorgos was in town. He had spared no expense in making sure the room would leave any visitor in awe.

Despite Pocasio's glare, Yiorgos leaned forward in his chair and pressed the intercom. "Send the Duke's envoy in."

Pocasio walked to a corner of the office, out of direct sight of the door. Yiorgos was used to the baron's idiosyncrasies, one being that he always stood off to one side of the room whenever Yiorgos had a visitor.

A few seconds later, the office door opened and a middle-aged man with graying hair entered. He was a slender man, taller than Yiorgos, well-dressed, with an aristocratic face. He squinted, as the windows behind the graf overlooking the capital, and the sun's angle was perfect to leave Yiorgos mostly in shadow.

"My lord?" he asked in a clear, respectful tone.

The graf rose slowly. "Mr. Foster," Yiorgos said in a pleasant tone. "Welcome to Melissia."

Foster walked toward the desk, sweeping the room with his narrowed eyes. "Thank you, my lord."

"Please, sit and we can talk. Would you like something to drink?"

"Coffee would be fine."

Yiorgos smiled. "Of course." he motioned to Pocasio. "My friend, Baron Iago."

Foster turned his head toward Pocasio. "My lord."

Pocasio stood there and said nothing.

Yiorgos pressed the intercom button and ordered coffee to be brought in. He sat and smiled at the envoy. "Now, Mr. Foster, what brings you all the way out here to Melissia?"

Foster sat. "My lord, Duke Vedet Brewer, has been asked to investigate the possibility of reclaiming worlds from the Jade Falcons. He and the First Hesperus Guards are in-system at this moment, monitoring the situation."

Yiorgos raised an eyebrow. "I gathered as much. How do we know you are truly from Duke Brewer?"

Foster slowly reached inside his jacket and pulled out an ivory-colored envelope. He reached out, offering the envelope to Yiorgos. "My introduction."

Yiorgos reached over and took the envelope. As he pulled it to him, he noticed the envelope was thick, high-quality, and expensive. On the front was written in a strong cursive hand,

Graf Yiorgos Laskaris. On the back, the envelope had been sealed with wax, with a seal pressed into the dried, blood-red dollop. He didn't recognize the seal, but it looked to be a well-crafted image.

He looked at Foster as he reached over and picked up a letter opener. The envelope parted reluctantly under the opener's edge, but it did so. Once he had put the opener back down, Yiorgos pulled out a sheet of folded paper as thick as the envelope. He opened the paper and examined the message it contained.

My Lord Yiorgos,

I am Duke Vedet Brewer of Hesperus II, and I greet you as a fellow noble. I arrived in your system a few days ago, and am currently monitoring the situation on Melissia. I am concerned about the current situation on-planet, and wish to help you and the rest of the council.

But while my First Hesperus Guards would give your forces a boost, I feel that would be a poor use of their talents. My people have informed me the Republic forces would react badly to the First's presence, and my comms people have picked up chatter among the Republic forces about using "The Final Option." We are not sure what this final option is, but we believe it could be a chemical or nuclear weapon. I do not wish to be the reason the Republic uses this weapon, but I cannot stand by and do nothing.

I have sent Hiram Foster as my envoy, to see how we can work together to win this war without the Republic using whatever this final option is. In a few days, I plan to publicly reveal my presence to both sides and offer myself as a neutral third party. In reality, you and I will work together to find and neutralize this final option and leave no opportunity for the Republic to use it. While I know the Republic rulers will have no trust in me, I plan to appeal to the people directly, and force their leaders to at least listen to me.

Publicly, I will be a neutral party trying to reach an agreement between both sides. In reality, you and I will working together to secure a victory for the Noble Council, one that will remove the Republic as a threat once and for all. I look forward to meeting you and the other members of the Noble Council in due time.

I spent a few months on Melissia many years ago, and I met your grandfather, Graf Priam Laskaris, and your father. Some of my best memories are from my time there, and I do not want to have them marred by a fool releasing a weapon of mass destruction. I hope that together, we can prevent that.

Respectfully,
Vedet Brewer, Duke of Hesperus

Yiorgos read though the letter twice, then looked up at Pocasio. "Has there been any mention of 'The Final Option' in Republic communications?"

Pocasio frowned. "Not that I know of. But there is a lot of Republic comms traffic that hasn't been reviewed yet."

"Review it all. I want evidence to prove or disprove such a thing exists."

"Of course, my lord. If you'll excuse me, I'll see to that right away." Pocasio walked to the office door.

Yiorgos leaned back in his chair and gave Foster an appraising look. "In the meantime, let's discuss what Duke Brewer can offer me and the Council."

CHAPTER 9

LOVELESS FOOTHILLS
JAHRESZEITWUNDER
MELISSIA
JADE FALCON OCCUPATION ZONE
FEBRUARY 5, 3151

The interior of the ST-46 shuttle was designed for luxury. The passenger bay had been overhauled and outfitted with paneling, carpeted floors, and comfortable chairs with heavy-duty harnesses for takeoff and landing.

The shuttle, *Brewer One*, was Vedet's personal shuttle. It was one of three flying in formation, surrounded by an aerospace squadron. He wasn't expecting trouble, but he wanted to show the Melissian Republic he was playing from a position of strength right from the start.

He'd spent the last couple of days reading through his envoys' reports, discussing them with Jennings and Kirk. After some discussion, he visited the Republic first. Foster's report from Europa showed Graf Yiorgos Laskaris was on the front lines, commanding a military operation to seize a pair of key villages near the southern coast.

The intercom next to his chair buzzed. "Your Grace, we have the runway in sight."

"Thank you," Vedet replied, then looked around the cabin. There were a half-dozen aides with him, experts on different area, and Bronislaw, sitting in a seat especially made for him.

Kirk had wanted Vedet to take an entire infantry squad with him as a bodyguard, but after reading Leeson's notes, had taken just his personal bodyguard, Bronislaw, with him. Bronislaw was from Elemental stock, a large man in both height and width. His face was scarred, the results of being a pit fighter. Vedet had first seen him during an underground pit-fighting match on Rapla, and had been impressed with the man's size and speed. Upon meeting with the pit fighter, Vedet had been even more impressed with the giant's intelligence, hidden behind a brutish face. It had been a simple matter to purchase Bronislaw's contract and bring him in as Vedet's personal bodyguard. Since then, the man had been a loyal and able defender.

"There are too many places for a sniper to hide out there," Bronislaw said, staring out the window. His voice was clear and deep, and his accent was flat and clipped.

"You think the Republic will try to kill me?" Vedet said in an amused tone.

"It is unlikely," Jennings said.

Bronislaw raised an eyebrow at the spymaster. "It is something I cannot dismiss out of hand. Their hatred of nobility is irrational."

"And misplaced."

Vedet nodded. "Which is why I am meeting them with just you as my bodyguard. It shows them I am not afraid of their words."

The Elemental looked back at Vedet. "I hope you are right. Colonel Kirk has the entire First ready to come down and either rescue you or avenge you."

Vedet raised an eyebrow. "I left no such orders."

The Elemental shrugged. "I suggested it to him before we left."

"Suggested?"

"He needed little convincing."

"Colonel Kirk was preparing a strike force to rescue, just in case," Jennings said. "Bronislaw made a reasoned argument to the colonel to prepare the entire First for an assault."

Vedet sighed. "Buckle up. We're landing."

The ST-46 landed on a ferrocrete runway a couple kilometers from the Republic's capital, the former Commonwealth fortress known as the Rock. On the ground, Vedet briefly spoke to the pilots, then returned to the cabin.

"There is a crowd waiting for us," Bronislaw said. He wore a business suit and had an assault rifle slung over his shoulder.

"The other shuttles?" Vedet asked.

"Brewer Two and Three are behind us and to our left and right."

"Good." Vedet looked at the others in the cabin. "Ladies, gentlemen," he said. "Let me make this clear. As far as the Melissian Republic is concerned, we are only talking to them. Do *not* mention the Noble Council except in general terms—do ask questions about them, however, and gather all the intelligence you can."

"Pass your observations to me when you can," Jennings said as he stood up.

Brewer felt the shuttle slowing to a stop. "Game time, people. Let's show the Republic we are worthy of their trust."

Bronislaw was the first one out, the bodyguard scanning the surrounding area before descending the shuttle's stairs and taking a spot next to them. Vedet was out next, looking around as he descended the stairs. What he saw was a rocky landscape with a few rough looking trees and patchy bushes. The colors were primarily grays and browns, with a few shades of faded greens mixed in. He felt the heat, despite the earliness of the morning. Not the most inviting place he'd seen, but better than some.

A half-dozen people were waiting for them about twenty meters from the shuttle. Vedet looked for Prime Minister Nicholas Mendez, but couldn't pick him out of the group. Behind them, a pair of large cargo trucks sat, guarded by several hovertanks.

He walked toward them feeling the warm breeze and dry air around them. It wasn't too unpleasant, but it was still early in the morning. In another couple of hours, it would be hotter and less pleasant.

As he approached, he could pick out the individuals of the reception committee. Three of the group were armed soldiers wearing camo uniform matching the surroundings—easily dismissed as security for the other three.

"Careful, Your Grace," Jennings said in a soft tone. "The leader is dangerous."

The woman in the middle was tall, lean, with a pinched face and a long neck wearing a white business suit. Next to her was a man, shorter than her, with short, platinum-blond hair and a solid face. Under the plain field uniform, he looked lean and fit, and the deep tan showed he was a man used to the outdoors.

When Vedet looked at the third member, he almost faltered. She was tall, lean, with long dark hair done up in a braid that hung over one shoulder. As they got closer, he saw her green eyes and a skin tone several shades lighter than his own, a darker shade of mahogany. For a fleeting moment, he thought she was Cassie, but the thought quickly dissolved, as she was clearly younger.

As they got with half a dozen meters, the woman in the middle stepped forward. "Duke Brewster," she said in a nasal tone. "I am Andrea Tippet, Republic Vice-Minister for diplomatic affairs."

Vedet felt a flash of anger at her tone and her calling him by the wrong name, but hid it with practiced ease.

Bronislaw loomed up behind him. "It is Duke Brewer, Vice-Minister. Not Brewster. I suggest you remember that."

Tippett glared at the bodyguard. She appeared to be unaffected, but Vedet noticed the uneasiness in her eyes, and had no doubt Bronislaw noticed it too. "Very well, Duke *Brewer*," she said, enunciating the name.

Vedet nodded once. "Vice-Minister. I am honored to be here."

"I suppose." Tippet spun on her heel. "Come, we'll talk at the Rock." She walked toward the cargo trucks with long strides, followed by all three soldiers. The other two looked back and forth between the vice minister and their guests, uncertain what to do.

"How charming," Vedet muttered.

"I take it shooting her is not an option?" Bronislaw asked in a whisper. Vedet noticed Tippet's aides snap their heads over to them at the Elemental's question.

"Not at the moment," Vedet muttered with a smile as he nodded to both of the Republic's officials. "But keep it open for future consideration."

The military man gave Vedet a critical look, but the woman raised an eyebrow, just like Cassandra used to do when he said something she thought was stupid. For an instant, Vedet saw Cassandra standing there next to Tippet.

"Your Grace," the man said. "Colonel Mason Nathanson, Melissian Republic Forces."

Vedet extended a hand. "Good to meet you, Colonel."

Nathanson took it, showing Vedet a strong but not overpowering grip. "Welcome to Melissia."

"Thank you." Vedet looked in the woman's direction, but she had turned and started walking back to the vehicles. "Who is that?"

"Callisto Mylonasa."

"Related to Baroness Cassandra Mylonasa?"

"The baroness was her mother."

"Was?"

"The baroness and her husband, Graf Laskaris, died in a vehicle accident the year before the Falcons invaded."

The grief slammed into Vedet, and he took a half step before firmly clamping down on his emotions. Automatically, he reached up and touched the ring hanging around his neck. "I'm sorry to hear that," he said, keeping his voice steady. "Who's her father?"

"That is a mystery, and also quite the scandal. Seems the baroness had Callisto before she married Graf Simon Laskaris. She never named the father, but the rumors are some visiting off-world noble was responsible."

Vedet felt his stomach clench. *Could it be?* "I see."

He saw a flash of surprise in Nathanson's eyes, followed by a thoughtful expression. He nodded and turned away. "We better get moving. The Vice Minister will not wait for us."

They started walking toward the vehicles. Nathanson walked beside Vedet, with Bronislaw close enough to cast a shadow over both of them. "You said the Graf and Cassandra were killed in an accident. What happened?"

"The car they were riding in went off a cliff near their home. I don't know if it was ever fully investigated. It was right before the Falcon occupation, and resources were limited. When Yiorgos assumed the title, he declared the investigation over."

"I see." Vedet made a mental note to have Jennings get a copy of the police report of the accident. "I'm surprised she's here, and not with the Noble Council."

"Callisto's not on speaking terms with Yiorgos, and from what little she's said about it, she doesn't like him."

Vedet nodded. "I suppose it was difficult for her, being a bastard child on a noble estate."

"I gather it was. She's never talked about it much, and after her mother died, there was nothing left for her on the Laskaris estate. So, she left."

Vedet nodded. He noticed the vehicles as they approached. Two were clearly security vehicles, with a pintle-mounted machine gun and occupied by armed soldiers. The other three vehicles were battered-looking wheeled APCs with a crude-looking "*MR*" on a shield painted on the side.

Tippet was getting into the first APC, followed by Laskaris, but when Vedet moved toward the vehicle, Nathanson stepped in front of him. "The second APC, Your Grace. It's not a good idea for VIPs to ride together."

Vedet nodded, but heard Bronislaw growl behind him. "Of course, Colonel. Lead the way."

The APC's interior had a feeling of age and hard use. There was enough room for Vedet, Jennings, Nathanson, and Bronislaw, but not much more because of the Elemental's size. Zabrina Leeson was sitting in the back of the compartment, and nodded to the Duke. "Smooth trip down, Your Grace?"

"It was all right," Vedet answered. "I read your report with interest." He glanced at Nathanson. "I just need to clarify a couple of points."

The colonel nodded. "I'll be back in a minute. I just want to make sure the rest of your party is loaded up." He stepped outside and walked away.

"Bronislaw, watch the door." Vedet walked to the front of the cramped compartment, followed by Jennings, and sat next to Leeson while the spymaster sat across from them. Jennings pulled a small device from a pocket, turned it on, and placed it on the floor between the, then nodded.

Vedet nodded to Jennings, then turned to Leeson. "What am I walking into?"

"The parliamentary coalition is under heavy strain. The Freedom Party doesn't want to have anything to do with you, but Mendez and the rest of the coalition will speak to you at least."

Vedet nodded. The Republic parliament was made up of eight political parties. The largest single party was the Freedom Party, the main source of the anti-nobility sentiment in the Republic. But while it was the largest party, it didn't have enough seats to form a government on its own. It was forced to form a coalition with three smaller political parties, and the price of the alliance was that the Prime Minister wasn't a member of the Freedom Party and several key posts, like Defense and Treasury, were held by minority-party members. Mendez had moderated the naked hatred of the nobility somewhat, but it remained just underneath the surface.

"What about Andrea Tippet?" Vedet asked.

"Hardcore Freedom Party member. Her boss is in ill-heath, so she's running the Diplomatic Affairs department in all but name."

"Yes, I got the impression she didn't like me," Vedet said dryly. "What about Nathanson?"

"Competent military leader, has no love for Tippet or the Freedom Party. Currently seconded to the Ministry of Defense after he refused to make a last stand in an indefensible position about ten days ago."

Vedet nodded. "What kind of reception should we expect?"

"A mixed one. Tippet hates your guts. Mendez will listen, but he has a hostile parliament to deal with—there are other parties that are even more anti-nobility than the Freedom Party."

"Then I will have to be charming," Vedet said with a smile.

"We have company coming," Bronislaw said.

Jennings picked up the device and stuck it into his pocket seconds before Nathanson climbed into the APC and pull the door shut. "Everyone's mounted up," he said, sitting across from Bronislaw. "Better buckle up."

Vedet pulled the harness into place and secured it around him. As he did so, he felt the APC come to life, and start moving with a lurch.

Alone with his thoughts, Vedet leaned back and closed his eyes. He reached up and touched the hidden ring. The memory came unbidden, as if it had been waiting for him.

"What about children?"

Cassie laughed. "Aren't we getting ahead of ourselves?"

"Seriously." He put his hand on hers. "What would we name them?"

She smiled and closed her eyes. The café they were sitting in was small and intimate, far off the beaten path. They hadn't gone public with their relationship, as neither cared for the press.

"Well?" he prompted her after a few seconds.

"Well," she said slowly, "for a boy, Anton or Leksi. For a girl..." She thought for a moment. "For a girl, the only one that comes to mind is Callisto."

He laughed. "Seriously?"

She shot him a hurt look. "It was my grandmother's name!"

He tightened his hand on hers in a reassuring manner and grinned at her. "If that is what you want, I have no problem with it..."

CHAPTER 10

THE ROCK
LOVELESS FOOTHILLS
JAHRESZEITWUNDER
MELISSIA
JADE FALCON OCCUPATION ZONE
4 FEBRUARY 3151

The conference room inside the Republic capital (if a fortress could be called a capital) had no personality. The furniture— chairs, the table, side tables and the painting on the walls— were the sort that could be found in any mid-price office store. The walls were cold gray, and the carpet was a darker shade of gray. Beyond the closed doors, guarded by Bronislaw, they could hear distant sounds of life elsewhere in the place they called "The Rock."

When they had entered the Rock, Vedet, Leeson, and Jennings had been escorted to the conference room by Nathanson and told to wait there. That had been thirty minutes ago, and nothing had happened since. Vedet recognized the tactic for what it was—a ploy to put him and his people off-balance. It was childish, but he would not take the bait.

While they waited, Leeson filled Vedet in on the current military situation. Jennings didn't take part in the discussion, but Vedet knew he was taking in everything and adding it to his files on the Melissian Republic. Wary of any listening devices, the three had discussed nothing else of importance.

Several more minutes passed before the door opened and Vice-Minister Tippet walked in, carrying several folders, followed by Callisto and Nathanson.

"Sorry for the delay," Tippet said in a tone that didn't hide her annoyance. She sat across the table from Vedet.

"The Prime Minister still busy?" Vedet asked in a calm tone.

He got a cool glare from Tippet. "He is. Now, why are you here? I thought you would be still lurking around Tharkad like a dog looking for scraps."

"I came looking to help."

Tippet leaned forward. "We don't need your help against the Council."

"Then you're a bigger fool than I thought."

The vice-minister reared back as she had been slapped. "You dare insult me?"

"Why not? You've been insulting me ever since we met."

"I've been treating—"

"—him like dung on your shoe," Nathanson finished.

Tippet shot him a hard glare, so she didn't notice Callisto reach into her pocket for something. Vedet watched her grip something for a second before pulling her hand out of her pocket and into her lap.

"Colonel," Tippet growled. "You are out of order."

"And the Duke is right. You are an idiot."

The vice-minister's face turned red. "Get out of here, you son of a bitch."

Nathanson looked undisturbed. "You have no authority over me."

Vedet looked over at Leeson. "You said the Republic has only six to nine months left? From what I've seen so far, I think six months is being generous."

That stopped the argument, and Vedet found three sets of eyes fixed on him from the other side of the table. He looked at Jennings. "Will you tell the good Vice-Minister what we have discovered about the Noble Council military?"

Jennings nodded and began detailing the "facts" about the Council's military strength. Five Council BattleMech battalions (They actually had less than three), ten mixed brigades of armor and infantry (In reality, only six brigades existed), and four VTOL regiments (In fact, the Council only had two). The numbers were inflated just enough to make them believable, but hard for the Republicans to easily confirm. The picture Jennings painted was a larger, stronger Council force, with more BattleMechs and soldiers.

As Jennings continued talking, Vedet noticed Tippet's expression slip into concern, Nathanson's thoughtful look, and Callisto's eyes narrowing in such a way it reminded him of Cassie whenever she thought someone was lying to her.

When Jennings was done, Tippet leaned back and said, "That's impossible!"

"Is it? Tell me, do you know the comings and goings of every DropShip that enters your atmosphere? The Council has three full BattleMech battalions, and a fourth is being formed even as you speak."

"Bah!" Tippet replied, waving a hand as if swatting a fly. "They can't match our zeal and strength of belief!"

"They don't have to beat you. They simply have to overwhelm you, like they just did at Gónnoi and Makrychori, especially if the quality of Republic commanders are as bad as the commander at Makrychori."

The vice-minister's face reddened. "How did—"

"We have technology you don't. We can monitor the entire front lines and do it close to real time. We know about the disaster at Makrychori, and how the Council now controls most of the Loveless and Broad Run Valleys. Your outposts in Grizano and Zarko are in danger of being cut off, and the Council is moving forces north, toward Karditsa Lake. They should be there in two or three days."

Tippet's mouth opened and closed, but no sound came out.

Nathanson broke in. "How sure are you of those movements?"

Vedet looked at Jennings. "Midori?"

"We've identified the Third Council Brigade and elements of the Fourth moving toward Karditsa Lake. In addition, the Second *Fylakes* Battalion has pulled back to Vitolishte, where the headquarters for the central front is."

"I don't believe you," Tippet whispered, her voice wavering.

"Consult with your own people." Vedet leaned back into his chair. "I can wait."

Nathanson rose. "I should pass this information along."

Just then the door opened, and a man in a business suit entered. Vedet raised an eyebrow as he recognized Prime Minister Nicholas Mendez.

"Andrea," he said in a brisk tone. "I thought I should drop by and meet with Duke Brewer."

Tippet shot Mendez an ugly look. "I thought you had meetings to attend."

The prime minister looked non-plussed as he closed the door behind him. "I'm letting Beryl chair a couple of the meetings. She needs the experience if she's going to be my successor."

The vice-minister expression darkened even more. "Why are you really here?"

"Why shouldn't I be?" Mendez sat in the chair Callisto vacated for him. "Thank you, Callisto. This won't take long." He looked at Vedet, leaned over the table, and extended his hand. "Duke Brewer, I am Prime Minister Nicholas Mendez, head of the Melissian Republic."

Vedet reached out and took the hand. Mendez's grip was strong, but controlled. "Prime Minister."

"Welcome to Melissia. I wish it was under better circumstances." Mendez released the handshake and sat back.

Tippet's face reddened again. "Surely you have other duties to attend to, Prime Minister?" she asked in a frosty tone.

Mendez smiled. "Not at the moment. In fact," He glanced at his watch. "It's nearly lunchtime. Why don't we take an early lunch? I can talk to the duke here without all the bells and whistles."

Tippet slapped the table with both hands. "Prime Minister, this is my area of expertise."

"Really?" Vedet said slowly. "I am offering you useful information, and you are refusing to see reality."

"Information?" Mendez asked. "What information?"

"He claims he has information on the Council forces," Nathanson said.

"Does he?" Mendez looked at Tippet. "Is there a problem with the information?"

"He's a *noble*," Tippet growled, spitting out the last word as if it was a curse. "He's just like any other noble—a blood-sucking parasitic scourge on the face of the universe. We should have—"

"Vice-Minister!" Mendez's voice cracked with anger and on his face was a mask of fury. "You're doing the Republic a disservice! Duke Brewer has come to us of his own free will and you're treating him as a common criminal! I instructed you *not* to offend the Duke and to bottle your hatred of the nobility."

Tippet sneered. "You are only in office on our sufferance."

"Really, vice-minister?" Callisto said. Vedet could hear Cassandra's echo in her tone, the tone Cassandra had used to dress down someone who needed it. "The next elections are in eight months. At the rate we're losing ground, the Republic will be no more in six!"

Tippet spun around, stood, and glared at Callisto. "You'd like that, wouldn't you?" she snarled. "Your brother's leading the Council and—"

"My *half*-brother is the last person I want in charge," Callisto growled. "He's a monster with little regard for human life. If I could kill him, I'd do it gladly."

Tippet's sneer deepened. "So you say. You're no better than you mother, a *pórni* who—"

Vedet rose from his chair. But before he could do anything, Callisto stepped forward and slugged Tippet across the jaw. The vice-minister stumbled back against the table.

"Call my mother a whore again," Callisto growled, "and you won't live to regret it."

Tippet pushed herself off the table. "You *skýla*!" she snarled. "I'll have you arrested!"

"You will do no such thing," Mendez declared.

Tippet turned toward the prime minister, and Vedet could see the large bruise forming in the vice-minister's cheek. "What?" she demanded flatly.

"I said you will not arrest Miss Laskaris. You provoked her by accusing her and her late mother of being whores, and then called her a bitch. If I was in her position, I'm not sure I would have stopped at just one punch."

"You're on thin ice," Tippet hissed.

"Speaking of ice, I suggest you go to the medical center and get some ice on that cheek. Colonel Nathanson, why don't you escort the vice-minister to the medical center? I'll take over here."

"I'm not—"

"That wasn't a request. You need to cool down, Andrea, in more ways than one."

Nathanson nodded. "A sound idea, sir." He looked at Tippet. "Vice-Minister, I think we should leave."

Tippet turned to face him and folded her arms. "As you've said, I'm not in your chain of command."

"Maybe not, but I can have soldiers here in less than five minutes and publicly drag you out of here. That's going to raise a lot of questions."

"You wouldn't *dare.*"

Nathanson's eyes narrowed. "My loyalty is to the Republic, not to a party or a single person."

"It's all right, Andrea," Mendez said. "Go take care of that bruise before it gets any worse."

Tippet turned to glare at the prime minister, then let her shoulders sag. "Very well, *sir*," she said stiffly. She stalked past Mendez and out of the room, followed by Nathanson.

Mendez waited until the door closed behind them before saying, "Callisto."

"Yes, sir?"

"Nice punch, but ill-advised."

"Sorry, sir."

"Don't be. Andrea should have known better. For someone who is supposed to be our second most senior diplomat, she shows a surprising lack of tact." Mendez turned to Vedet. "I'm sorry you had to see that, Your Grace."

Vedet sat slowly. "That's all right, Prime Minister. I was impressed with both Miss Mylonasa's physical skill, and the vice-minister's ability to take a shot like that."

Mendez wave a hand in dismissal. "It hasn't been the first time, and I am sure it won't be the last." He turned to look at Callisto. "Come join us, my dear."

Callisto came over to the table and sat next to Mendez. The prime minister leaned forward. "Andrea is an arrogant *skýla*, but she knows how to keep operational security. Only a dozen people know of your arrival, and only half of them know who you are. Now, let's talk about why you are here and what you can offer us."

CHAPTER 11

THE ROCK
LOVELESS FOOTHILLS
JAHRESZEITWUNDER
MELISSIA
JADE FALCON OCCUPATION ZONE
4 FEBRUARY 3151

The guest quarters assigned to Vedet were functional, and somewhat comfortable. Before lunch arrived, Jennings distributed several white-noise generators around the quarters to foil any listening devices. Bronislaw searched the suite—living area, compact kitchenette, bedroom, and bathroom—for any unpleasant surprises. After nothing was found and the white-noise generators were in place, Vedet, Leeson, and Jennings sat in the living area.

"You were not understanding Tippet's hatred of the nobility," Vedet said.

"Tippet's the highest ranked Freedom Party member in the cabinet," Leeson replied. "While she had the same view of the nobility as most of her party, she's made it personal. She and Mendez are butting heads all the time. He can't get rid of her, because if he did, the Freedom Party would pull out of the coalition, and the government will collapse."

"Would they do such a thing during the middle of a war?" Jennings asked.

Leeson pursed her lips for a few seconds. "I think they would. One of their major positions is to eliminate all the planet's nobility and strip them of their family fortunes for 'redistribution to the masses.'"

"That explains why the Council came into being," Jennings said.

"What is your opinion of Nicholas Mendez?" Vedet asked.

"A decent man trying to do a good job while trying to balance sanity with what the hard-core Freedom Party fanatics want," Leeson replied. "If given a choice, he'd leave the nobility alone."

"But it isn't his choice," Vedet said.

"It isn't. He's trying to mute the worse of it, but he's under pressure to enact executive orders that will invalidate the noble titles and seize their lands and property."

"Even though they're losing? I don't know if I should be impressed with the Freedom Party's blindness to reality, or scared of their single-mindedness."

"It should be both," Bronislaw replied. He stood near the front door, looking like he was part of the plateau. "Such people need to be challenged in a Circle of Equals."

Vedet shrugged. "That's the problem with these kinds of people. They're not warriors."

The Elemental scowled. "*Surats.*"

There was a knock at the door. Bronislaw moved to it, placing his body between his employer and whoever was outside before opening it. He opened the door, looked, then stepped back. "Visitors, Your Grace."

Callisto Mylonasa and Mason Nathanson walked in. Callisto looked nervous, looking around the room before she settled her gaze on Vedet.

Vedet stood slowly. "Miss Mylonasa, Colonel Nathanson. How may I help you?"

Callisto looked at Nathanson, the back to Vedet. "Can I speak to you, Your Grace?"

"About what?"

Callisto took a deep breath. "It's a personal matter."

Vedet tilted his head. "What sort of personal matter?"

He could see she was trembling. Nathanson placed her hand on her shoulder to steady her. "A question of parentage, your grace."

Vedet nodded slowly. "Bronislaw, scan them."

The sensor wand was already in the giant's hand, and he quickly ran it up and down the visitors' bodies. "No weapons or explosives on either."

Vedet motioned them toward an empty couch. "Please, sit. Would you like something to drink?"

Callisto shook her head. She still looked anxious, but she had it under control. The colonel's expression was more restrained, but he kept his hand on her shoulder as they walked over to the couch and sat. Callisto looked at Jennings and Leeson, then looked back at Vedet.

The duke sat down and leaned back. "You look very much like your mother."

Callisto jerked. "You knew my mother?"

Vedet nodded. "When were you born?"

"December 28, 3021."

Vedet nodded. "That fits."

"What fits, Your Grace?" Jennings asked.

Vedet watched Callisto through half-closed eyes. "Ask what you want to ask."

Callisto inhaled slowly. "Are you my father?"

The duke sat there, finding the right words. "I very well could be."

The answer took Callisto by surprise. "You don't know?"

Vedet shook his head. "Cassandra was many things, but she was never a *pórni.*"

Callisto nodded her head slowly. "I have to know. Did you love her?"

"With all my heart and soul."

"Then why did you leave her?" There was a tone of sadness in her voice, with some bitterness.

"It was not by choice, it was *politics.*" He spat the last word out, then was silent for a few seconds. "Blame Graf Priam Laskaris. His son Simon needed a wife, and Cassandra was the one he chose. Her father was in debt, and Priam purchased all of it to force him to agree to the marriage. He also had the backing of the local nobility and the Margrave."

Vedet closed his eyes for a moment, then opened them. He reached inside his collar and pulled the necklace with the ring on it out. "I proposed to her with this ring, begged her to come with me, to Hesperus II. She was crying when she said no. She had a duty to her family, and as much as she loved me, she couldn't leave."

"You couldn't do anything?"

"I tried seeing her again the day I left, but my security detail hunted me down, dragged me back to the DropShip, and sedated me until we were out of the Melissia system. Once I was back on Hesperus II, I was grounded—I couldn't leave the planet for several years, and all communications I made off-planet were monitored. Despite that, I tried several times to contact her, but she never replied."

"You didn't know about me?"

Vedet inhaled slowly. "No. If I had I would have come back, back for both of you, and damn the consequences."

"She told no one who my father was," Callisto said. "Not Simon, and not Priam, or anyone else. Oh, they suspected, but she never confirmed it." She looked down at her feet, then up at Vedet. "Only after Mother died, and I went through her possessions did I realize why she said anything. She kept your letters, you know."

Vedet couldn't hide her surprise. "She did?"

"And your gifts." She reached up under her collar and pulled out a necklace she wore. Vedet caught his breath as he recognized the small diamond-and-emerald-encrusted pendant. "The only times I ever saw her wear this was when she was angry with Simon. He always seemed to get the message."

Vedet stood and walked over to Callisto. "May I?"

Callisto nodded, and Vedet lifted the pendant and looked at it carefully. He smiled when he spotted the small break in the gold wiring holding the gems together. He lowered it and looked down at her. "I brought that for her in a small jewelry shop in Europa's Artisan District. The same place I bought this ring from." He touched his necklace.

She nodded. "DelMicio's." she dropped her head. "The Artisan's District didn't survive the Falcons' occupation."

"I'm sorry to hear that."

She looked up at him. "I don't know why she never told me about you."

He tucked the ring back into his tunic. "She didn't want to make you a target."

She snorted. "I expected you to deny you're my father."

Vedet was silent for a few seconds. He walked back to his chair and sat down. "Cassandra wasn't someone who slept around. If you say you might be my daughter, I have to take it seriously. Would you be willing to submit to a DNA test? You look so much like Cassandra, but I want to make sure you are her daughter."

Nathanson's expression darkened. "You don't believe her."

Vedet sighed. "I have learned over the last few years that trust is a fragile thing. I want to believe that Callisto is Cassandra's daughter with all my heart, but I can't take it at face value."

The colonel rose to his feet. "You god—"

"Mason!" Callisto said, grabbing his arm. "He's right. If I was him, I would be suspicious." She looked at Vedet. "I'll do it."

Vedet nodded, then turned back into the room. "Midori."

"Yes, Your Grace?"

"Go find the medic we brought with us and request his DNA ID kit. Tell him we need it for a demonstration."

"Yes, Your Grace." Jennings stood and headed for the door.

"Are you sure about this, Callisto?" Nathanson asked as he sat down again. Vedet noticed the concern in his tone.

She nodded. "Everything's fine."

"While we wait," Vedet said. "I have a couple of questions. What was it like growing up?"

"Difficult," Callisto replied. "When the Laskarises found out Mother was pregnant with me, they were furious. They demanded she abort me, but she refused. My grandparents, now free of their debts, backed her. Graf Priam tried to declare her incompetent, but Simon stepped in and said he would support both of us. By the time things were sorted out, I was born."

She took a deep breath and composed herself before continuing. "I was raised by my grandparents until I turned thirteen, then was sent to live with mother and stepfather." She took a breath. "Simon... well, Simon tolerated me. He was never cruel or abusive, but he was never warm to me either. He kept that for Yiorgos." She snorted. "Spoiled him."

"Yes, I've gathered you don't like Yiorgos."

Anger flashed in Callisto's eyes. "Simon may have never been father of the year, but he was a damn sight better than either his father or son. Priam had three mistresses and died in the arms of the youngest one. Simon had my mother and no mistresses. But Yiorgos?" She closed her eyes and shuddered. "He thinks he's God's gift to women. You can blame that attitude on Priam—Simon was busy with his duties and mother was more concerned with me than him, so Yiorgos spent a lot of time with his grandfather."

She hesitated, then with another deep breath, continued. "I think he was behind the accident that killed mother and Simon, and when I started asking questions, someone tried to run me down on the street in broad daylight. Yiorgos dismissed my concerns and told me to leave it alone."

"Do you have any evidence he was behind the accident?" Vedet asked.

"Nothing I can prove, but that's Yiorgos for you. Always the suspect, never the culprit."

Vedet made a mental note to look into Yiorgos' background. "I'm sorry."

She waved him off. "No matter, but it's my turn to ask a few questions about you."

Vedet spread his hands. "Go ahead."

"When and how did you meet my mother?"

Before Vedet could answer, the suite door opened and Jennings stepped inside. "I have the kit."

Vedet nodded, then said to Callisto. "It's up to you. I won't force you to submit."

"Are you sure this is a good idea, Callisto?" Nathanson asked,

"I need to show him," she said. "As he said, trust is a fragile thing."

Jennings walked toward them with a belt pouch in one hand. Callisto looked at the pouch. "How is this going to work?"

"The procedure is simple," Jennings replied, removing a cylinder the size of a writing stylus from the pouch. "I'll use this tool to scrape a few cells from inside your cheek, then place the cells into the reader." He held up a compact noteputer. "I already linked the reader to Melissia's DNA database."

"How long will it take?"

"We should know the result within five minutes."

Callisto nodded slowly. "I'm ready."

Jennings took the stylus. "Open your mouth, please."

She did so, and Jennings scraped the tool inside her mouth, then inserted the stylus into a port on the reader and tapped a few buttons on the screen. "It'll take a few minutes for the results."

They waited. Vedet asked Callisto. "Nervous?"

She shook her head. "I know who I am."

The scanner in Jennings' hands beeped. He looked at the screen. "Miss Laskaris' identity is confirmed, and her maternal DNA matches Grafina Cassandra Laskaris with a ninety-eight point three-five percent certainty. There is no paternal DNA match in the database."

Vedet smiled as he stood. "That's enough for me. Callisto, come here."

Callisto stood and walked over to him. Vedet hugged her, stroking her hair and said. "I wish I'd never left your mother. I wish I tried harder to come back."

She relaxed in his hold. He looked down and saw tears leaking around her closed eyes. "I Me too, Papa. Me too."

After Callisto and Nathanson left, Vedet sat in his chair, a thoughtful expression on his face. "Midori."

"Yes, Your Grace?"

Vedet opened his hand, the one that had stroked Callisto's hair, revealing several hairs on his hand. "Collect these, please."

Jennings gave Vedet a questioning look, but came over and using a pair of tweezers, carefully collected the hairs and put them into a small bag. "You don't trust Callisto?"

"I want to, but I can't. DNA profiles can be hacked. When we get back to the JumpShip, I want a DNA comparison started. My DNA profile is on file in the DropShip's database."

"What about Cassandra's DNA?"

Vedet fingered the ring under his tunic. "I have a lock of her hair on the dropship. I want a full DNA profile on all three samples. If Callisto is my daughter, then I will love her as a father should."

"And if she isn't?"

"I don't know."

CHAPTER 12

For the trip to Europa, Melissia's capital, Vedet had used the *Blade's Edge*. There were several *Fury*-class DropShips operating in Council territory, so it would be harder for Republic intelligence to connect Vedet to it. Also, he wanted to speak to the Council from a position of strength, and the *Blade's Edge* was more of a statement than *Brewer One* was.

After another two days of meetings, Vedet and his team had made some progress, then gone back to the JumpShips and met with his military commanders. A small military team was dispatched to the Rock to supply data from the Guards' observation satellites. In addition, plans were drawn up to place several Guard *Kampfgruppen*—Battle groups—on the ground to act as a buffer and to help the civilians caught in the crossfire.

Now, Vedet and a couple of his senior military commanders were heading for Europa and a meeting with Graf Yiorgos Laskaris. Vedet wasn't sure of his feelings about the man. For right now, he needed to keep a clear head and unbiased opinion about the man and his plans.

Which was why he was sitting in the *Blade's* conference room with Thomas Kirk and Helen Goreson, listening to Jennings' detailed briefing on the Noble Council.

"The Council is made up of fifteen nobles, but only four members hold any real power." The spymaster touched a button on a portable holo pad sitting on the table and it sprang to life, showing a full-body image of a young man wearing a uniform that was close to, but not exactly a LCAF dress uniform. He had short blond hair, light brown skin, blue eyes, and a round face that looked nothing like Callisto's features. "Yiorgos Laskaris, Graf of Northen Jahreszeitwunder. He's the senior noble on the planet, and the only one of his rank."

"Weren't there other grafs?" Kirk asked.

Jennings nodded. "There are two other families that hold graf rank on Melissia. The Papandreouses fled when the Falcons invaded, and have not been back since. The Tolivers stayed, but Graf Victor Toliver died during the revolt against the Falcons' garrison, and the heir, a nephew, hasn't stepped forward yet to claim the title."

"See if you can find him," Vedet said. "Continue."

Jennings nodded. "On the surface, the graf is charismatic and has some military skill. When the previous Council head, Graf Toliver died in battle, Laskaris stepped in and assumed the leadership role of the Council and the military. Under his leadership, the Council forces have seized most of the Broad Run River Valley and large sections of the Chortiatis Hills in the north."

"Under the surface?" Vedet prompted.

"Under the surface is a man who is ruthless, arrogant, and cold-blooded."

That sounds a lot like how my enemies see me, Vedet thought. *And they may have a point.*

"Per your request," Jennings continued, "my team has been digging up everything they can on the Council members. Miss Callisto was right when she said Yiorgos was always the suspect, never the culprit. We found a lot of red flags around him."

"What sort of red flags?"

"Let's start with his time at college. When the Falcons invaded, he was ranked in the lower third of his class and spent almost all his time partying. He was spending a lot of kroner and had plenty of friends and hangers-on. But a few of his associates were not college-party types, but known members of the Malthus Syndicate."

"Which is?" Goreson said.

"Organized crime," Vedet replied with disgust. "They tried several times to infiltrate Hesperus II, and my security forces had to be 'undiplomatic' when dealing with them. They have their fingers in everything—drug dealing, illegal gambling, prostitution, and loan sharking— among others."

Jennings nodded. "Exactly, Your Grace."

"So, he was in their clutches?" Kirk asked.

The spymaster hesitated. "The evidence shows Laskaris was more of a partner than a victim."

"I take it by the fact he's not in jail, they pinned nothing on him?"

"Apparently, he had several layers of cut-outs between him and the actual operations and whenever the police thought they were making progress, bodies of suspects slammed the door in their faces. Still, the police made several connections to Laskaris when the Falcons invaded. Among the buildings destroyed were the police evidence warehouse and police headquarters. Interestingly enough, the evidence warehouse was not near the fighting."

"Convenient," Kirk muttered.

"Very," Vedet said, as Callisto's words came back to him: *"Yiorgos thinks he's God's gift to women..."* "Yiorgos is reportedly a womanizer. Any traction there?"

Jennings looked pained. "There were several cases of unwanted sexual advances or harassment, but the charges were quickly withdrawn. Two other cases fell apart because the complainants turned up dead or missing."

"Okay, this guy is lucky or vicious," Goreson growled. "And if he's running with the Malthus people, I'm betting on the latter."

Vedet scowled. He had his faults, but abusing women was not one of them. He'd always treated women he had relations with in the past with respect and affection, and parted on good terms. Only Cassie had been anything more than a casual affair, and no other woman could match her. "I suppose he had an alibi in both cases?"

Jennings nodded. "Of course."

Vedet grunted. "Awfully convenient, don't you think?"

"Sounds like a slippery character," Goreson said.

Kirk nodded, his face stony. "We can't trust him, Your Grace."

Vedet nodded. "That's clear. Anything else, Midori?"

Jennings nodded. "We obtained the report of the accident that killed Graf Simon Laskaris and his wife. I had both Dr. Ginley and Hauptmann James read the report separately, and they both agree the accident is suspicious."

Vedet found his anger rising, his fingers cradling the ring around his neck. Ginley was the senior civilian doctor with the task force, with some experience in pathology. James was the commander of the Guards' MP company and had accident-investigation experience. "They think it was murder?"

"They both agree the accident has unanswered questions."

"And where was Yiorgos at the time of the accident?"

"He was in the capital, five hundred kilometers away, at the time of the accident, halfway through a five-day whoring and drinking binge."

Vedet's anger was simmering now. "And Graf Toliver's death?"

"The circumstances of his death are also suspicious. During the battle for Markam Bay, the graf's *Thunder Hawk* squared off against a Falcon *BattleMaster* in a ravine near the main port. Heavy ECM made communications almost impossible, and it wasn't until after the battle did anyone realize the graf was missing. Both combatants were found dead, the Falcon pilot from his wounds, and Graf Toliver's cockpit had taken a PPC hit."

"What's suspicious about that?"

"The *BattleMaster*'s PPC was non-functional when both 'Mechs were found. I dispatched Bale and Ramsey to Europa and infiltrate the storage facility where it's being stored. They checked the PPC, and both agree it hadn't been functional for some time. That was confirmed by the 'Mech's maintenance records we downloaded. Whoever shot the Graf, it wasn't the *BattleMaster*."

Kirk frowned. "So, someone else killed Graf Toliver."

"It appears so."

"Who discovered the scene?" Vedet asked.

"Graf Laskaris."

"That's really convenient," Goreson said. "I may not be the brightest bulb in the bunch, but even I see who the number one suspect is."

"And what 'Mech does he pilot?" Vedet asked.

"A *Titan II*."

"Which has a PPC," Goreson said. "The more I hear, the less I like Laskaris."

"We still have to deal with him," Vedet said.

"Just count your fingers after you shake his hand and don't turn your back on him."

"I agree with Helen on this," Kirk said. "Laskaris sounds like a monster who'll stab us in the back the first chance he gets."

Vedet scowled. "I won't argue the point, but for now, we're going to have to at least appear to be working with him. We don't have to trust him, but we do nothing that make them suspicious."

Goreson sighed and leaned back in her chair. "All right, but if he gropes me, he's losing that hand."

"I'll pass the word along," Vedet said dryly. "What about the others?"

Jennings tapped a button on the holo pad, changing the image to a tall, lean woman in her mid-forties, a mature beauty with ash-blond hair and gray eyes. "Baroness Josette Kerr. She's considered the second-in-command of the Council, but she doesn't have anywhere near Laskaris' authority. She handles the Council's economics, and oversees the movement of money."

"Someone we can reason with?"

"Possibly. Her overriding concerns are her family. As long as they're not threatened, we can deal with her."

"I'm not the type to go after people's families," Vedet said. "She doesn't strike me as someone who trusts Laskaris either."

"She's aware of his background. Her family, which includes two teenage daughters, is on an isolated and fortified island three hundred kilometers from Europa, with a strong security force for protection."

"Maybe we should monitor them?" Goreson said.

"It might be wise to do so," Kirk said.

"Midori, will that be a problem?" Vedet asked.

"We can work it into our operations."

"Do so, but take no actions against the island. If Laskaris tries anything, then we can step in, but let's not reveal our secrets."

"Yes, Your Grace." Jennings changed the image to a short, rotund man with a nervous expression, a pale complexion and wearing an ill-fitting suit. "Baron Alban Dyhr. He's in charge of communication and propaganda for the Council, mainly because no one else wanted the job. One of his sons was executed by the Falcons, and he hates them with a passion. The Republic seized his lands, and he escaped with the rest of his family one step ahead of their security forces, so these days, the Republic are number one on his grievance list."

"He could be a problem," Vedet said.

"Possibly. But restoring his lands could go a long way toward quieting his anger." Jennings exhaled. "The last member of the four has me the most concerned."

The holopad image was replaced with one of a man with forgettable features and no expression, wearing an old, but clean and pressed suit. "Baron Iago Pocasio. Beyond the basics, he's an enigma. No family, no friends, few associates. He's been off-word multiple times, and we think he's the Council's main mercenary recruiter. We have sightings of him consulting with Laskaris' Fylakes troops several times."

"Fylakes?" Kirk asked.

"Laskaris' personal troops. Greek for 'Guardians.' Considered elite troops, but they're rarely used in battle. They're mostly used as internal security and pacification troops."

"So Pocasio's head of internal security?" Goreson asked.

"We think so. Most of the Council members don't have clearly defined areas of responsibilities, so the clashes between council members are common."

Vedet rested his hand on his chin. "Maybe that's by design. If the council is fighting each other, that means there's no one challenging Laskaris for control."

Jennings nodded. "A reasonable conclusion. But getting back to Pocasio, I think he's more than just internal security. I firmly believe he's my counterpart on the Council."

"Then I think we'll treat him as such," Vedet said. "Anyone else?"

"There's one other, though she's not officially part of the Council." The image changed again to show a tall, thin woman with a blue-green Mohawk and a scarred face. "Colonel Tricia Maldonado, head of the mercenaries the Council hired. She was one of Bannson's Raiders' senior officers until Bannson was taken out by his own people and the rest of the unit imploded in the aftermath. She's wanted on a few worlds for war crimes, and the Republic has her on their 'To Kill' list."

"Dig up everything you can on the mercenaries' chain of command." Vedet glanced at the clock on the bulkhead. "We have forty-five minutes before we land. Let's make some plans to follow when we sit down with the Council."

CHAPTER 13

EUROPA
JAHRESZEITWUNDER
MELISSIA
JADE FALCON OCCUPATION ZONE
8 FEBRUARY 3151

Vedet was prepared to hate Graf Yiorgos Laskaris on sight.

Yiorgos entered the conference room, wearing a plain field uniform with no insignia. He walked with a confidence of someone secure in his authority, but there was a welcoming light in his eyes swept the room before they fell onto Vedet.

"Your Grace!" Laskaris said with a wide smile and hands held wide. "Welcome to Melissia!"

Vedet and the others with him—Foster, Kirk and Goreson—rose from their chairs and nodded. "Graf Laskaris."

The conference room was in the Margrave's Palace, on the edge of the capital. Originally a well-finished room, it had been a victim of the Falcons' lack of interest in anything that didn't serve their purpose. The walls were bare of paintings, and the conference table and chairs had seen better days.

Trailing the Graf were Dyhr, Kerr, and Pocasio, all wearing civilian suits. Behind them Colonel Maldonado wore tight leather clothing and boots, and her dark eyes swept the room, marking targets. Pocasio was doing them same thing, but his gaze was deeper and more penetrating.

After introducing each other's teams, Laskaris motioned toward the chairs. "Let's get down to business." Each group sat on opposite sides of the table. Bronislaw stood against the wall behind Vedet, large and immobile. The graf looked at the bodyguard for a few seconds, then smiled and looked at Vedet.

"Now," Laskaris said. "I was admittedly surprised when your man Foster here showed up with your letter. I thought you were a hunted man."

Vedet shook his head. "The Commonwealth needs every soldier it can get its hands on. I was dispatched to see what was happening out here in the old Melissia Theater. Imagine my surprise when I found the Falcons had abandoned several planets we visited. We thought they had retreated here and made a quiet entry to secure the planet. We were astounded that there's no Falcon presence here on Melissia."

"They left little behind," Baron Dyhr growled. "And they didn't last long after we rose up and killed them all."

"But I find you fighting this Melissian Republic."

"Damn Freedom Party!" Dyhr snarled. "A bunch of neo-communist—"

Laskaris placed a hand on Dyhr's arm. "Alban, calm yourself. His Grace is here to help." He looked at Vedet. "What do you know about the current situation here on Melissia?"

"Just what we've gleaned from the news reports we've picked up," Vedet replied.

"Good. Then you know we are in a fight for our very way of life."

Vedet glanced at Foster, then back at the Graf. "Has there been any attempt to negotiate with them?"

"They refuse!" Dyhr snarled. "As far as they're concerned, we nobles are no better than parasites!"

"Their own ideals blind them," Laskaris said, his tone reasonable. "They see us as a threat to their success."

"So there's no common ground?"

"Of course not," Baroness Kerr replied, sounding tired. "They want to get rid of the nobility entirely, take away our titles, and seize our lands."

Laskaris shook his head. "Josette's right. They're no longer interested in being part of the Commonwealth, and the nobility is a reminder of that old way of life."

Vedet noticed Maldonado frown and filed it away. "So, it's war."

Laskaris nodded, his expression grim. "It's a war of survival, one we must win."

"From what I've seen, your forces are doing well."

"We have them on the back foot. We have pushed the front lines thirty kilometers in the last month, but we're short of trained soldiers. Most of our military are volunteers, with Colonel Maldonado's mercenary BattleMechs stiffening them. We have the weapons, and we've been fortunate that the Republic's military leadership is mostly incompetent, but their soldiers are better trained than ours."

Vedet looked at Kirk. "I think we could help there, right, Thomas?"

"I believe we can lend the Council a few training instructors," Kirk said with a nod. "What sort do you need?"

"Basic training for starters," Laskaris said. "And advanced trainers in the fields of infantry, medical, and technician."

Kirk rubbed his chin. "Basic training isn't too difficult. We could find maybe two dozen who can cover that. The advanced training's not so clear-cut."

"Maybe a half-dozen for each specialist field?" Goreson said.

Kirk nodded. "I think we can do that. We could also add in some training equipment."

"That would be most welcome!" Laskaris said with a smile.

Vedet returned the smile. "Let's discuss a few things."

They returned to the *Blade's Edge* in the late afternoon, when Jennings had spent all day using the DropShip's comm equipment to intercept and decipher the Council's military radio traffic.

The Spymaster was waiting for them in the conference room. "Welcome back, Your Grace."

Vedet nodded and stepped aside, allowing Kirk and Goreson past him and into the compartment. "Good to be back. Any problems?"

"No, it's been quiet."

"I need a drink," Kirk said.

Vedet turned and tapped an intercom button on the bulkhead next to the hatch. "Drinks to the conference room," he said, the voice echoing over the DropShip's loudspeaker system.

Goreson dropped into a chair and put her head back. "I never knew talking could be so exhausting."

"You've sat in your share of conference meetings before," Kirk said.

"Yeah, but they were shorter, and Pocasio sat there and just stared at us. Never said a word."

"Enough," Vedet said.

Foster walked into the compartment. "The graf seems to be in a good mood."

"We're offering to train his troops," Kirk replied in an annoyed tone.

"There's more to it than that," Vedet said. "The Council is getting its supplies from somewhere. Weapons and supplies aren't cheap, so when you assign our people as drill instructors, instruct them to check the equipment the council issues their soldiers and see if they can get an idea about where it was manufactured."

Kirk nodded. "That should be doable."

Vedet looked at Jennings. "How has SIGINT been?"

"Better than expected. It'll take some time to go through everything and separate out the useful bits of data, but it should give us a better idea of the Council's capabilities and intentions."

"Good. Any progress on Peacekeeper?"

"We should have a location for initial landings within forty-eight hours."

"Better."

"Neither side is going to like us butting in," Kirk said.

"I'm not doing it to please either side," Vedet replied. "I'm doing it to win the population's hearts and minds while dealing with both sides secretly. As long as each one thinks I'm going to throw in with them, they'll tolerate what we're doing."

"That's going to be tricky," Goreson said. "Personally, I'd rather sit back and watch them butt heads."

"I agree," Goreson said, lowering her head so she could see everyone. "Our choice is between a bunch of screaming fanatics and a bunch of stuck-up nobles. No offense, Your Grace."

"None taken," Vedet said.

Foster walked over to a chair and sat. "Laskaris is a control freak," he said. "He doesn't like it when things happen that he can't control."

"Good. Have you tried talking to other members of the Council?"

"Not really. The four do most of the talking for the Council. Well, three of them. I've never heard Pocasio speak at any meeting I've been at."

"Talk to the others and get a feel for their position. Are they just going along with the rest, or do they want something else?"

"You want to know how the rest of the Council feels about Laskaris?"

"In a roundabout way. Kerr doesn't want him anywhere near her daughters, Dyhr is blinded by hate and Pocasio's an enigma. I want to know how the rest feel."

"It'll take some time."

"Don't rush it. Better to do it slow and steady."

"Foster nodded. "Yes, Your Grace."

There was a knock at the hatchway. "Drinks, Your Grace."

"Good," Vedet said, getting to his feet. "Enough about today. Let's plan for tomorrow."

CHAPTER 14

FILLYRA
JAHRESZEITWUNDER
MELISSIA
JADE FALCON OCCUPATION ZONE
11 FEBRUARY 3151

Fillyra was a small city overlooking the Titarisios River, north of the valley of the same name. Sitting on a bluff and accessible only by a few roads from the east, the city had declared itself neutral in the war between the Republic and Council, and with neither side having the resources nor the time to conduct a siege, it had been left alone.

Which made it the perfect place for the Hesperus Guards to use as a base for Operation Peacekeeper.

Peacekeeper was necessary for Vedet's plans for the planet. If he was going to win the hearts and minds of the population, Vedet needed the Guards to show the citizens another option besides the two warring factions.

It was why he was sitting in a news studio, at a desk, while technicians were moving about, checking lights and camera angles. He had gone through twenty minutes of make-up, and now all that was left were the final preparations.

He saw Jennings walk toward him. Once he was close enough, the spymaster leaned into his ear and whispered, "Leeson and Foster have let the faction leaders know what's happening."

Vedet nodded. This was going to be a balancing act—continuing to make each side believe he was dealing with them alone while Kirk, Goreson and the others won over the population. To ensure that, Vedet was going to move between the two, talking and listening, looking for cracks in each others' armor he could exploit. The data the Republic was getting from the Guards about Council troops' movements—just enough to be useful without giving them a major advantage—was a greater short-term benefit than the instructors Vedet had lent to the Council. He didn't trust either side, but Vedet didn't intend on this speech being for them, but the citizens trying to survive.

Jennings stepped back just as the floor director, a young woman with wide eyes from too much coffee and too little sleep, stepped over to him. "We'll be on air in thirty seconds."

"Thank you," Vedet said.

The city council had been surprised when Vedet contacted them, and were leery at first about being tangled up in the war they had so far avoided. But after Vedet promised his troops would not interfere with the running of the city and would protect it from both sides, they had reluctantly agreed.

The day had seen the First Hesperus Guards land, unload their DropShips and immediately set about improving the city's defenses. In the morning, small combined-arms *Kampfgruppen* would move out and start patrolling both sides of the river. Already, plans were being made to build forward bases to extend the Guards area of control. Now, it was evening and while the city prepared for any sort of backlash, Vedet was about to announce his presence on the plant.

He looked down at the speech in front of him. It wasn't long, but it contained all the points he wanted to get across.

He looked up, just as the floor director was starting a five-second countdown from beside the camera with her fingers. *Four, three, two, one—*

He waited a beat longer before he nodded at the camera. "Good evening, citizens of Melissia," he said, his tone somber. "My name is Vedet Brewer, Duke of Hesperus."

He let that sink in for a second, then continued, "I was sent out here to see if the Falcons are truly gone." A lie, but one that couldn't be discovered for a while yet, if ever. "It appears they are, so I came here to Melissia, the district capital, to see if I could aid in rebuilding."

He let his face slip into sadness. "But what I found was a planet at war. Both sides have grievances, some of which are legitimate. However, while the people of Melissia fight and die in battle, other forces out there are moving against the planets the Falcons have abandoned."

He let the sadness morph into seriousness. "While the Falcons are gone, both the Ghost Bears and Hell's Horses are still out there, and they will come—maybe not today, not tomorrow, but sooner than later. Warlords are also rising to rule their planets, and seek other worlds to bring under their control."

Seriousness became resolve. "To survive the darkness swirling around us, Melissia needs to be reunited. I have enacted plans to make this happen. The first is to deploy my own Hesperus Guards to Melissia. Starting tomorrow, they will act as a buffer between Council and Republic forces, patrol for bandits, and help people who need it with medical and food aid. We will not be replacing the local governments, but we will aid them with crowd control and shield those people who are helpless from those who would do them harm."

He nodded to the camera. "I call for both the Republic and the Council to send a representative to a mutually agreed location, where we can together resolve this war and plan for Melissia's future. Thank you for your time, and God bless Melissia."

"And cut!" The floor director yelled.

The camera light went out, but Vedet waited a few seconds longer before relaxing. "How was that?"

"Perfect!" the floor director said. "You should have been a newscaster!"

"I prefer to make history, not read it."

"Well, it was more than good enough. I daresay about a third of the population saw it and by tomorrow, twice as many will have seen it." She turned. "All right, thirty minutes' break, then we start the interview!"

Vedet waited for a tech to come over and unclip the microphone he was wearing, then stood. The day had been long, and it wasn't over yet. In a half-hour, he was going to have an interview with the local news anchor team to showcase Vedet Brewer the man. The interview was to be wide-ranging, no holds barred, a tough, but necessary measure to show he wasn't the man his enemies made him out to be. That would be broadcast tomorrow evening.

He walked over to Jennings. Bronislaw stood nearby, his looming presence creating an island of emptiness around them. Despite that, he kept his voice low. "How long before we get a response from the citizens?"

"A few minutes yet. Are you sure this is going to work?"

"You said neither side wants to sit down with the other and talk things out."

Jennings nodded. "The Council thinks it's winning, and the Republic refuses to think they can lose. Each side believe they'll crush the other with your help. Right now, talks are not high on their list."

"Which give us a chance to get the population on our side."

"Yes, Your Grace."

"Any word on the Toliver heir?"

"No. Either he's staying deep in shadows or he's dead."

"With Laskaris around, it could be either one. If we could find him, we could use him as a counter to the graf."

"We're still looking, Your Grace." The spymaster glanced at his watch. "But right now, eat something light and get something to drink. The interviewers are going to be tough and thorough. Are you ready?"

"I'd better be."

CHAPTER 15

SOUFLI
JAHRESZEITWUNDER
MELISSIA
JADE FALCON OCCUPATION ZONE
14 FEBRUARY 3151

"Delta Echo-Six to Delta Six."

Hauptmann Walter McWalsh held his hand up to silence Soufli's mayor. "Excuse me, ma'am," he said, tapping his headset to open the channel. "Go for Delta Six."

"We have a column of armor headed toward us from the west. Looks like company strength, light armor and infantry."

"ID?"

"Still looking... Got it! Looks like they're Flakes! Council troops!"

"Damn it!" McWalsh growled. "Hold one." He looked at the mayor. "Get your people to shelter. There's an incoming column of Council soldiers. If there's a fight, I want the population out of the way."

The mayor, a short, squat woman with short white hair and a permanent scowl, nodded. "Give them hell, son."

"I'll try." He turned and ran for his vehicle. The Manticore II was one of a pair in McWalsh's lance, along with a pair of DI Schmitt tanks. "Start her up!" he yelled as he crossed the distance. The driver, Colman, was leaning against the side of the tank, while Parson, the main gunner, was half inside the forward hatch. Both soldiers moved, Parsons dropping into the tank, while Coleman scrambled up the front glacis toward the driver hatch.

"Delta Six to all Delta elements!" he shouted into his radio. "Condition Monsoon!"

Around him, the rest of *Kampfgruppe* Delta scrambled to action. Soldiers raced for their vehicles, while others shut hatches and began the process to get their vehicle moving.

"Delta Foxtrot-Six to Delta actual. Where do you want us?"

Walt clambered up the side of his Manticore. "As soon as we set up a blocking position, come up, but stay out of sight unless I call for you. I want to see if we can get them to back down without revealing your presence."

"Copy, Delta actual." the voice sounded resigned.

"You know the ROE, Foxtrot. Unless they shoot, we can't do anything."

"Doesn't mean we have to like it."

Walt reached the turret hatch and dropped into the opening. As his feet hit the deck, the Manticore roared to full power. He slapped the hatch control and dropped into his chair. Quickly strapping in, he plugged his comms into the tank's system. "Delta Six to Hesperus Command."

"Go for Hesperus Command." The voice was eerily calm.

"We're at Soufli, and we have a column of *Fylakes* headed our way!"

"Copy. We are vectoring a fighter flight your way, ETA is ten minutes."

"Copy, Command. We are moving to intercept."

"Where we going, Boss?" Coleman asked.

On a side screen, Walt pulled up a map of the area and focused west of the town. "Delta Three-Six. What's the ETA on those Flakes?"

"Maybe ten minutes."

"Keep an eye on them. They change directions, let me know."

"Copy Six."

Delta Six to all Delta elements. We're going to set up a blocking position at coordinates Gamma Six-Three-Seven-One. Delta Command Two, set up north of the highway. Delta Command One will set up south of the highway. There's a low ridge there, plenty of cover. Delta Bravo and Delta Charlie will set up along the ridge, on both sides. Delta Echo, make sure they don't have any friends around. Delta Foxtrot. Stay behind us. You're our ace card if they don't see reason."

There was a round of "affirmatives" and the *Kampfgruppe* moved out.

From the Manticore II's open turret, Walt watched the approaching *Fylakes* move toward them on the four-lane highway. He counted sixteen vehicles—mostly APCs and a lance of Scorpion tanks—drive along in a single file coming in their direction. "Delta Three-Six, this is Six. I'm counting one-six vehicles. Can you confirm?"

"Affirmative, Six. One-Six vehicles is the entire package."

The *Kampfgruppe* was spread out on a couple of rises on either side of the highway. Delta Bravo and Charlie—a platoon of Gray Death Strike armor and a company of mechanized infantry—were scattered along the ridge. Delta Foxtrot was a hundred meters behind the ridge, as a reserve.

He activated his throat mike. "Attention, approaching Council forces! Halt!"

The column slowed and suddenly scattered in a pre-arranged formation, becoming a staggered set of two lines and continued advancing. It looked impressive, but the veteran armor officer mentally noted a few mistakes as they shifted.

"Who is this?" a nasally voice demanded.

"Hauptmann Walt McWalsh, First Hesperus Guards. Who is this and why are you here?"

"*Lochagos* Dwight Lawson, Second *Fylakes* Battalion. What are you doing here?"

Walt translated the rank in his mind, the result of a crash course in *Fylakes* ranks. "I asked first, Captain."

Lawson snarled, "We had reports of a bandit group operating out of Soufli."

"Sorry, we've been in Soufli for the last six hours. There are no bandits there now."

"What do you mean 'there're no bandits there now'?"

"Well, we heard an SOS from the town, and arrived just as a bandit gang was attacking. They didn't last long against us. We were cleaning up when you showed up."

"I don't believe you."

"I'm sorry you feel that way, Captain. I'm sure my superiors will forward my report to your superiors."

"You have no right to interfere with Council business!"

"And what business is that?" Walt growled. "I was at Vathi a day after one of your 'security sweeps.' I saw what you Flakes did—we helped to bury the bodies. You're not doing that here."

"How dare you! We—"

"Are jackbooted thugs who like pushing people around," Walt replied, his tone icy. "News flash, *Captain*. Soufli is under our protection. You have five minutes to turn around or I'll make sure you and your company regret it."

He dropped into the command chair. "Parsons, I want you to aim for a spot in the median strip with the HPPC, fifty meters in front of the Flakes. Fire on my direct command only." He switched channels. "Dottie, I want you ready to lay a burst of RAC fire across that highway twenty-five meters in front of the Flakes. Fire only if you see Parsons fire."

"On it," Sergeant Doratheria Hillman, commanding of the DI Schmitt in Walt's section, replied.

"What about us, boss?" Staff Sergeant Theo Carmichael, commander of the other section of Walt's platoon, asked.

"Stay quiet for now. I don't want to give him any more intel than I have to."

"Copy, boss."

"Delta Six, this is Angel Three-One. We are one minute out and coming in from the east. What are your orders?"

Walt smiled and rose out of his hatch again. "Copy, Angel. I want you to come in fast and low on either side of the highway. The Flakes only have a few autocannons and machine guns. Make one pass and hang around for a few minutes."

"Copy, Delta."

Walt switched back to the channel with Lawson, catching the Flakes captain in mid-rant. "—are not part—"

"Captain," Walt said. "Shut up and listen closely. You will stop, turn around and leave now, or you're never leaving. Parsons, fire."

The Manticore II's Heavy Particle Projection Cannon fired. The bolt of man-made lightning slammed into the median strip, digging a shallow hole in the ground. As the bluish energy faded, Dottie's twin rotary autocannons ripped a line in the ground parallel to the advancing Council force, sending dirt and chips of ferrocrete into the air. The advancing vehicles slowed, shocked at the display. But they weren't breaking—yet.

"Delta Six, Angel Three-One. We are making our pass now."

Walt smiled. "Copy, Angel. Delta Foxtrot, Showtime."

The *Fylakes* were shaking themselves out of their shock when Foxtrot—a *Gauntlet*, *Storm Raider*, and two *Firestarters*—appeared on the ridge line. As they came into view, a pair of *Stingray* aerospace fighters shot though the sky overhead, the noise of their passing overpowering everything else.

"Your choice, Captain. Retreat and live, or fight and die quickly."

The *Fylakes* slowed, then came to a complete stop before all their vehicles began moving backward. Several of the treaded vehicles threw up clods of dirt in their haste. There was no collisions or sideswiping as the armored vehicles tried putting distance between them and the suddenly deadly threat the Guards displayed.

"Look at the Flakes run!" someone shouted on the radio.

"Keep the comments to yourselves!" Walt growled. "We will not laugh at anyone who doesn't want to die against a superior force!" No one else commented.

After a couple of hundred meters, the *Fylakes*' front line of vehicles made a hard turn. The left side of line turned ninety degrees left, the right side turning ninety degrees right, as if they were on a parade ground. The APCs making the turns slid to a halt, then started moving again, turned back in the direction they had come from. The Scorpions, their turrets pointing in the ridge's direction, finished their turns and roared after the APCs. The first line passed through the second, which was still backing up, still not colliding with each other. Once the first line had passed completely though the second line, the second line repeated the first's action, turning ninety, stopping, then turning away to follow their comrades. The Scorpion's turrets were facing over the back of their vehicle, a mild but still sobering threat.

"We'll be back, Hauptmann!" Lawson growled over the radio. "My superiors will hear about this! Next time, you won't be so lucky!"

"We'll be waiting, Captain," Walt replied in an even tone. "And I'll pass your message onto my superiors."

As the *Fylakes* continued retreating, Walt said, "Delta Echo. Send someone to keep an eye on them. If they even twitch back in our direction, I want to know about it."

"On it, Six."

"Angel Two-One. Looks like that pass of yours was enough to send them running. Thanks for the helping hand."

"Not a problem, Delta. Glad to help."

Walt dropped back into the Manticore's turret and switched channels. "Delta Six to Command. Flash priority. I need to speak to the general ASAP."

CHAPTER 16

EUROPA
JAHRESZEITWUNDER
MELISSIA
JADE FALCON OCCUPATION ZONE
16 FEBRUARY 3151

Baron Iago Pocasio strode down the hall toward Laskaris' office. His expression was bland, but inside he was angry.

The source of his anger was directed toward two nobles—Duke Brewer and Graf Laskaris.

In Brewer's case, Pocasio knew what he was—a power-hungry man looking for a chance to regain power. Pocasio had never believed Brewer's assurances that he was here to help the Noble Council against the Republic. He had no proof, but he was sure Brewer was also in contact with the Republic, playing both sides against each other, to leave neither side in a position to oppose him when his forces swept in and took control.

But what really galled him was that the duke was succeeding. Units from the Duke's Hesperus Guards had already made their presence known on both side of the border in the last four days. Several bandit groups—including two under Pocasio's control—had been wiped out, and security troops from both sides had been denied entry into settlements for "security checks." Soufli had been an especially black mark—now it was being used as a base for Brewer's people!

But most of his anger was directed at the graf. Pocasio had hated all nobles—even before he'd assumed the identity of

Iago Pocasio many years ago. Yiorgos Laskaris was everything Pocasio hated about the class—self-serving, egoistical people who thought an accident of birth made them superior to other people.

He nodded to a pair of Council military officers as they passed him, his expression carefully neutral. The real Iago Pocasio had been dead long before Gray Monday, long before the elimination of the HPG communications system that had made his mission redundant. There was no ComStar to back him up, no force of ROM agents to use to further the plan that had been in motion for twenty years. What the Republic didn't destroy, the Sea Foxes bought, buying out ComStar as if they were merely a company, and not the holy guardians of technology and a new future for humanity.

His original mission, to influence the local government into backing ComStar research, was replaced with a more important one—establishing sanctuaries for the faithful remnants of Blake's vision. With the Order shattered, there was a need for places where they could rest, reorganize, recruit, and rebuild in secret. Now with the Inner Sphere falling into chaos, Pocasio's mission took on a new urgency. Melissia would be the core of a new ComStar in this part of the Inner Sphere, a place to spread their influence once again.

And while he had been making steady, if slow progress toward the goal, the appearance of Vedet Brewer was not making his already complicated job any easier.

A pair of *Fylakes* guarded the Graf's office. Both soldiers gave Pocasio a careful going over with their eyes, looking for anything suspicious. One of them stepped forward, a hand on the slung machine gun they each carried, the other holding up a detection wand drawn from a thigh holster. "Good morning, Baron."

Pocasio slowed and sighed. "*Sminias*," he said, holding his arms out to his sides and stopping a meter in front of the soldier. As the sergeant used the wand to scan Pocasio's body for any weapons, the baron wondered for a hundredth time why the Graf insisted his personal guards used Greek rank terms instead of English or even German terms. He noticed the second guard was softly speaking into his radio. Probably warning the graf of his arrival so the man could stop "discussing" things with his aides and get his pants back on.

It was a distasteful assignment, but if Melissia was to become a place for the Order to rebuild, they needed a planetary leader that could be controlled and manipulated. Neither the Tolivers nor the Papandreouses had someone that could be molded to the Order's purpose, but the Laskarises did. Pocasio had worked his way into the Laskaris' circle of associates, and became a known person to the young Yiorgos. It took a few careful conversations over the years to direct the young noble down the right path for Pocasio's needs, aided by Yiorgos' rake of a grandfather.

In college, Yiorgos Laskaris was a hedonist, not caring about much about money, as long as he was the center of everything. With Pocasio's help, Laskaris had formed an alliance with the Malthus Syndicate to take over the college drug market on Melissia. But the operation had gotten too big too fast, and Pocasio had stepped in to clean up the "problems" before either the police or the syndicate got wind of the disaster. Not all the bodies were ever found.

It was during this time that Pocasio saw the hedonist become less pleasure-seeking and more ruthless with illegal activities. Laskaris took on a more active role in the operations and showed a willingness to do what was needed, including murder. In a matter of months, he had full control of the entire illegal drug market on Melissia and the respect of the syndicate.

After college, the alliance between the Graf and the crime syndicate grew stronger, expanding into other areas. Somewhere along the way, Grafina Cassandra Laskaris had discovered her son's dealings and threatened to go to the police. It had been Pocasio who had stepped in and arranged the "accident" that had killed both the graf and grafina, leaving Yiorgos as the new graf. When the graf's half-sister had asked questions about her mother's death, Pocasio tried killing her, only she had escaped and gone to ground a few weeks before the Jade Falcons had invaded.

Once Melissia was theirs, the Falcons had sorted the population into two categories; "useful" and "deadweight." They placed the useful population into enclaves and left the deadweight to fend for themselves. Most of the nobles had been driven out of the cities to their estates, and resistance to the Falcons was met with overwhelming firepower and ruthless suppression.

It was during this time that the young graf started showing another side of himself. Using the skills he had gained as a crime lord, Yiorgos began forming alliances with other nobles on the planet, seeking to establish a resistance. Graf Toliver had been among the first to join the alliance, and the two of them had worked for several years to recruit, train, and equip a resistance force. Yiorgos' partners had supplied numerous weapons, equipment, and trainers for the task.

When the Jade Falcon garrison left Melissia, leaving a small paramilitary force behind, the nobles moved quickly. After three weeks of fighting, the Falcons had been annihilated, and the nobles had come out on top. Graf Toliver had died in the last battle of the war—at the hands of his fellow graf—leaving Laskaris as the highest-ranked noble on the planet.

But then the population in the Falcon enclaves, having been subjected to several years of Clan brutality, had rejected the nobles and had taken it on themselves to set up their own government, the Melissian Republic, and demanded the nobles disarm and give up their titles and property. War had broken out, and now the Republic was on the back foot, losing ground and looking defeat in the face.

The *Sminias*—sergeant—stepped back. "You can go in, my lord."

The baron nodded and went into the office. The outer office was designed to awe and overwhelm any visitor with the power of the owner. Every piece of furniture—desk, chairs, side tables, the paintings on the wall—were all high-end pieces, each one worth enough to feed and clothe a family for a whole year. The carpet was thick and tightly woven, a mix of gold, blue and sea green that reminded Pocasio of the Melissia seas.

The secretary—a stacked redhead this month—was settling in at her desk and still adjusting her blouse. "Baron," she said in a smoky voice, "The graf will be done in a moment."

"I'll wait."

A few seconds passed, and one of the graf's "aides" opened the inner office door and walked out. Her uniform—in name only, as no self-respecting soldier of any Inner Sphere military would be caught dead in such an outfit—was still askew, and her glazed expression told Pocasio all he needed to know about the what the Graf had been doing. She smiled at him, and the baron scowled in return. "The Graf will see you now."

Pocasio stalked past her, already banishing her presence from his thoughts. Inside, the office was the same as the outer, and more. Here the furnishings were antiques and the paintings should be—and probably had been—in museums. A single large window to Pocasio's left looked out over the street and the buildings across it.

Laskaris was sitting behind the desk. "Iago!" he said with a smile. "What do you need to see me about?"

Pocasio's smile didn't quite reach his eyes. "The latest reports on Brewer's activities."

"What have his people done now?"

"He's extended his area of control. He is basically in charge of about four hundred square kilometers of territory centered on the city of Fillyra. The latest base they've established is in Soufli."

Laskaris scowled. "Yes, I heard Lawson's report. While embarrassing, he did the right thing to retreat. I refuse to lose men in a battle they can't win."

"He's interfering in our plans!"

Laskaris nodded. "Do you have any suggestions?"

"Yes! Send Maldonado and two-thirds of her 'Mechs to crush them!"

"No."

"Why not?"

The graf chuckled. "My friend, you are valuable to me, but military matters are not one of your strengths. I could do as you suggest, but I won't. First, Maldonado and her mercenary *apóvrasma* would get mauled by Brewer's people."

"That 'mercenary scum,' as you just called them, are the reason we're winning this war!"

"Iago, please." Laskaris held up a hand to cut off Pocasio. "We both know the Guards are better trained, have more support forces such as aerospace fighters and battle armor, and more cohesion in their training and knowledge. Maldonado could win, but it would cost us. I'm not some Republic diehard who is going to destroy my force in a fit of pique."

"But Brewer is—"

"Second, it would alert the Republic as to just how large our BattleMech contingent is. We've been fooling them into thinking we have only a battalion and a half of older 'Mechs. To do as you suggest, we would lose that advantage. And last, I want Brewer's troops under my command. With them, I could form the core of our new military around them."

"They're loyal to Brewer!"

Laskaris nodded slowly. "So we must first see if we can eliminate Brewer."

Pocasio's scowl deepened. "Killing him won't be easy."

"You'll find a way. Just must make sure they blame the Republic for it."

"And in the meantime?"

"We'll continue negotiations with him. If we can come to an agreement before you're ready, we'll keep it as an option. How long do you think you'll need?"

"It'll take a week to arrange, maybe longer."

"As soon as you can make it."

"I'll see what I can do."

"Good. Oh, by the way...have you made any progress in finding Victor's nephew?"

"No," Pocasio replied with another scowl. "We know one of the Free Guilds smuggled him onto the planet a couple of months after Victor's death, but we've found no trace of him since then."

"Pity," Laskaris said. "I want him found. We don't need two grafs running around confusing things, do we?"

Recognizing the tone of dismissal, Pocasio turned and left the office. He didn't look at either the aide or the secretary on his way to the outer door. Once he passed the two guards at the outer door, he pulled out his perscomm and dialed a number from memory.

"Yes?" a male voice said.

"It's me," Pocasio said, his stride not slowing. "Meeting now, top five, and activate Arcadia."

"Arcadia?" the voice asked. "Are you sure?"

"Yes."

"Understood. Meeting place Victor, half-hour. Arcadia is active."

Pocasio ended the call and pocketed his perscomm. Twenty years of work was in danger of being destroyed. Eliminating Brewer would be difficult, but doable. However, they had to be ready to cover their tracks in case it blew up in their faces. Nothing could be allowed to point in their direction. As far as anyone else was concerned, Pocasio and his people were never here.

CHAPTER 17

Vedet used the *Evening Star* as his base of operation for several reasons. The main reason was to make it clear to both sides that he wasn't looking to rule the territory his Guards were patrolling. In fact, no one in the local governments—Council, Republic, or neutral—had been replaced and Vedet had ordered his troops not to interfere with local affairs unless innocent lives were at stake.

Every shipboard morning, when he was onboard, Vedet would get an update on what was going on Melissia. When he wasn't on the *Evening Star*, he was shuttling between the Rock and Europa, discussing the planetary situation with each side.

Vedet floated into the conference room for the daily briefing. "What do you have today?" he asked, floating over to a chair and sitting, making sure his magnetic soles were firmly on the floor. Kirk and most of the Guards' senior officers were already there.

Jennings tapped a couple of buttons on a large holopad. The picture that came up was a 3D image of a large part of Jahreszeitwunder. The Republic sector was in red, the Council territory was in blue. A sliver of green sat between the two factions, the territory the Guards were actively patrolling.

"As of this morning, we are patrolling an area of five hundred square kilometers, from near the source of the Broad Run east to Soufli. We're getting inquiries from towns and villages in a thousand square kilometers requesting our presence."

"How long until we can extend our range and start helping these other villages?"

"Another day or two. We're moving infantry and armor into the four forward bases we have—that'll allow both *Kampfgruppen* we have at each base to go out at the same time. That'll increase our range and cover more ground. In two days, we should be able to double our patrolling range."

Vedet nodded. "Public reaction?"

"Overwhelmingly positive. News teams are swarming the area, talking to the residents about what we're doing. A few people have suggested that maybe you should be in charge of running things, and there have been a few requests for interviews."

"What about our friends in the Republic and the Council?"

Jennings sighed. "The Freedom Party are foaming at the mouth, demanding that you cease 'interfering in planetary matters.' They've tried twice in the last two days to pass declaration of war against you and the Guards, claiming you are the 'vanguard of a Commonwealth invasion force,' but Prime Minister Mendez has blocked both attempts from reaching the floor for a vote."

"Good for him."

"I think it's more a fear you'll side with the Council if he allowed them to be voted on."

"And the Council?"

The spymaster frowned. "Surprisingly mild, considering what *Kampfgruppe* Delta did to one of his *Fylakes* companies."

Vedet snorted. "I thought Hauptmann McWalsh showed great restraint in not wiping them out to the last man."

"Yes, Your Grace. In fact, the graf has invited you to spend the weekend with him at his estate outside of Europa."

"Has he?" Vedet leaned back and folded his hands. "He doesn't seem upset we embarrassed some of his toy soldiers?"

Jennings grimaced. "He claims there was an error in the transmitted orders to the *Fylakes* company."

"You believe him?"

"We have the recorded transmissions. The orders were quite clear."

"Sounds like he's overlooking this small disagreement."

"That's not normal for him, is it?"

"The man has an explosive temper. He executed the last Council commander who retreated without orders. As far as we know, the *Fylakes* captain McWalsh faced down is still alive and in charge of his company."

Vedet lowered his head so his chin rested on his hands. "He still wants the alliance."

Jennings nodded. "It appears so. If for no other reason, so you don't side with the Republic."

"But is that all it is?"

"Your Grace?"

"I feel as if there's a knife pointed at my back and he's the one holding it."

"You think he'll betray you the first chance he gets?"

"Don't you?"

"It is a definite possibility."

"No, make that a certainty."

"You think he's an actual threat to us?" Kirk asked.

Vedet shook his head. "He thinks *I'm* the threat. Me and the Hesperus Guards. He may have numbers, but he knows our people are better trained, better equipped, and can cripple his forces if we so choose to. The Guards would be an immediate boost to either side's military."

"Sir," Kirk said, "I think you need extra bodyguards."

"Absolutely not. If I show up with extra bodyguards, both sides will start wondering why."

"Your Grace," Kirk said, his voice tight, "I don't care what they think. My duties include keeping you alive."

"Not now. We have to keep both sides believing I could side with them."

"May I make a suggestion?" Goreson asked. "We could assign members of Echo Company to Your Grace as military aides."

Echo Company was a demi-company that acted as a first assignment for MechWarriors recruited into the Guards, and it acted as a ready reserve and replacement pool for the rest of the battalion. On paper they were part of the First's 'Mech battalion, but because of their status, didn't have permanent assignments.

"I think that's a good idea," Kirk said quickly. "It would give us extra sets of eyes, add extra guns, and would fit in with the rest of the teams." He looked at Vedet. "Your Grace, I must insist on the extra security. Bronislaw is good, but he's only one man."

Vedet looked over at the Elemental. Bronislaw shrugged. "As long as they know I am in charge and stay out of my way, I have no problem with extra security."

The duke sighed. "Fine. Assign them." He looked around the table. "Have our drill instructors come across any evidence as to where the Council is getting his military supplies from?"

Jennings nodded. "Our people examined the weapons and equipment 'for quality control.' They found a third of the equipment was manufactured on Medellin, and the rest of it has Medellin custom stamps on it. Which makes sense, as several Medellin corporations have commercial ties to Melissia, ties that were broken by the Falcons and the contracts declared void by the Republic when they occupied Europa. It's easy to trace most of the supplies to those corporations."

"Good. Midori, have you located that Toliver heir?"

"No, Your Grace. He is proving to be ... elusive."

"Assuming he's even still alive," Kirk muttered.

"Graf Laskaris believes so. He has ordered more men into the search for him."

"Keep at it," Vedet said. "Anything else?"

"Not at this time, Your Grace."

Vedet rose. "I'll go down and talk to the Republic tomorrow. Maybe I can give Mendez something he can wave at the Freedom Party."

CHAPTER 18

NORTH LOVELESS VALLEY
JAHRESZEITWUNDER
MELISSIA
JADE FALCON OCCUPATION ZONE
24 FEBRUARY 3151

"Delta Echo Three-Three to Delta Six! Condition Tsunami! Repeat, Condition Tsunami!"

Walt McWalsh's head jerked up from his map reading. *Kampfgruppe* Delta was moving down Highway Seven, heading south. "Delta Six to Echo Three-Three. Confirm Tsunami!"

"Tsunami confirmed. Feeding visual."

Walt's head turned to a side monitor as it flickered to life with a push of a button. The video was shaky—a helmet camera on a soldier who was emotional tended to be shaky—but what he could see chilled him. At least a dozen APCs were sitting on edge of a town and the picture steadied enough for him to make out the Republic insignia on the side of several of the trucks.

He glanced back at his map and saw the town in question was Gildfield Gap, some ten kilometers south of him. He glanced back at the video as a party of Republic soldiers came into view, escorting a much longer number of civilians. All had their hands on their head, and from the jabbing the guards did with their rifles, the civilians were prisoners. The camera swung around to reveal a *Stinger* and a *Griffin* in Republic colors standing in the town square.

"Damn it," he hissed. Tsunami was code for civilians being assaulted by either the Republic or Council forces. "Delta Six to All Delta Echo elements. Can you confirm Three-Three's Condition Tsunami?"

"Echo Three-Two here. Tsunami confirmed."

Walt felt himself grow cold. "All Delta Echoes, if you have eyes on what's happening, send me the video feed. Delta Foxtrot, take Charlie and get to Gildfield Gap."

"Copy, Six." The 'Mech lance, with the APC-mounted Gray Death battle armor, could get there faster than he could.

"The rest of you, we're heading for Gildfield Gap." He switched channels. "Delta to Command, I have a Condition Tsunami."

There was silence for a few seconds, then the gruff voice of General Thomas Kirk come on the channel. "Confirm Tsunami."

Walt tapped a couple of buttons. "Sending live feeds now."

The Manticore II was picking up speed. While he waited for Command to respond, he ran a checklist of the tank's different weapons systems. He was almost done when Kirk said, "Delta Six, this is Command. You are to try to get them to leave peacefully. If they don't leave, or fire on you, I authorize you to open fire, ROE Beta."

Walt exhaled. "Copy, Command. Talk first, then shoot, ROE Beta."

"I'm vectoring in Charlie and we're spinning up a reserve company. ETA is twenty minutes on both."

"Copy, Command. We're on it."

Leutnant Lisa Lee loved being a MechWarrior.

Her family had been MechWarriors for generations, and Lisa had been brought up on stories of the modern-day knights. The reality was much different, but she had always seen herself as a descendant of those armored and mounted warriors of old.

Now, she and her lance were racing down Highway Seven toward people who needed help. Her *Gauntlet-A* was running flat out at over ninety kilometers an hour on the ferrocrete road, but the rest of her lance—Harrigan's *Storm Raider*, and the

Commisos' *Firestarters*—were quicker and ranging ahead. Even the Gray Death armor, riding inside hover APCs, was moving faster than she was. She briefly considered using her 'Mech's Myomer Accelerator Signal Circuitry to make up some of the ground, but rejected it as being unnecessary.

She looked up and saw dark clouds on the horizon. *Hope that isn't a metaphor for what's coming*, she thought.

McWalsh had given her the orders and instructions for the upcoming confrontation. Rules of Engagement Beta boiled down to, "Don't fire unless you're fired upon, or civilians are in immediate danger," and "try and not to kill anyone if you can avoid it."

She saw Staff Sergeant Harrigan's *Storm Raider* slow. The rest of the unit also slowed. "Foxtrot Six," Harrigan said in a raspy voice. "I can see smoldering ruins a kilometer ahead. Looks like a ranch or farm."

"Copy," Lisa replied, "keep moving."

"Understood." The *Storm Raider* picked up speed again.

"Charlie Six, send a squad to look at the ruins to make sure there's no one there needing our help."

"Copy," Staff Sergeant Bonnie "Boom-Boom" Barton, the battle-armor leader replied. "Charlie Three, look at those ruins as we pass."

"Copy, Boom-Boom."

"Contact!" Harrigan shouted. "*Commando* at fifteen hundred meters, bearing three-twenty, on an intercept course!"

"Contact!" One of the Commisos twins called out. Lisa could never tell which twin was doing the talking. Val and Vash Commisos were identical, right down to their *Firestarters*. "*Arctic Fox*, coming in on a bearing fifty-seven degrees, seventeen hundred meters out!"

"Spread out but stay within support range!" Lisa ordered. "Foxtrot Six to Delta Six. We have BattleMechs approaching, ID unknown."

"Copy. Give them a verbal warning, but continue advancing."

"Copy, Six."

The two forces continued closing the distance and Lisa felt her unease growing. "Attention *Commando* and *Arctic Fox*!" she said over several general comm channels. "This is Leutnant

Lisa Lee of the Hesperus Guards. Identify yourself and state your business!"

Almost immediately, both light 'Mechs broke off their advance and angled away before turning and running away.

"Six, do we pursue?" Harrigan asked.

"Negative. Our goal is to get to Gildfield Gap ASAP. Charlie Six, belay that order to send a squad to those ruins. I'll pass word back to Delta Six and let him deploy help."

"Copy Foxtrot Six. Charlie Three, back in line."

They raced past the smoking ruins of what looked like a farmhouse. Lisa hissed as she saw the damage, two half-walls were the only identifiable parts of the structure left, as everything was else was blackened and charred. She prayed there was no one alive left in the building. She had a larger mission. Activating her radio, she told McWalsh about the farm and the possibility of survivors.

Several minutes later, Gildfield Gap came into view. Nestled in the shadow of a mountain pass, the town consisted of several dozen buildings, two-and-three story white stucco affairs. Between Foxtrot and the town, the area was open grassland, with scattered trees and a few rocks large enough for infantry or vehicles to hide behind, but not 'Mechs.

The Republic 'Mechs towered over most of the buildings. Besides the *Commando* and *Arctic Fox*, there was a *Stinger* and *Griffin*, along with a dozen military vehicles. As soon as they came into view, the town came alive as the soldiers in it responded to their appearance.

"Foxtrot Six to Foxtrot and Charlie. Let's slow it up and see if we can get them to come to us." *And give the rest of the* Kampfgruppe *a chance to catch up before we have to fight,* she thought. They were several minutes behind her, and she needed to buy some time. "Attention Republic forces! This is Leutnant Lisa Lee, of the Hesperus Guards. State your business here!"

"This is not your concern," a harsh feminine voice replied.

"Who is this?" Lisa demanded.

"Major Plenosi, Republic Internal Security Battalion Three. This is an internal security matter and not your concern."

"Echo Three-Two to Foxtrot Six!" The scout's voice was tense with horror. "They're lining up people in the center square and—and I think they're about to execute them."

Lisa felt a chill go down her spine. "Major Plenosi, tell me you are not executing civilians."

"That is not your concern."

"Well, Major, I'm making it my concern. Stop what you're doing immediately and withdraw."

"Or what?"

"Or We're going to kick your ass up into your teeth."

"You can try!"

The *Griffin* and *Stinger* ignited their jump jets and rose into the air on plumes of plasma. As they did so, the *Arctic Fox* went left, the *Commando* went right to outflank her lance. "Charlie Six, head for the town, flank speed! Foxtrot Three and Four, go after the flankers! Don't open fire unless they fire first!"

"On it," the Commisos said in unison.

"I have the *Commando*," one said.

"I have the *Arctic Fox*," the other said. Both *Firestarters* darted away, one going in each direction. The four hover APCs immediately shot forward at full speed.

"Delta Six!" she shouted into her radio. "We're under attack!"

"Careful," McWalsh said, "they may try to provoke you."

"They're doing a good job of that! Foxtrot Two, you have the *Stinger*! I'll take the *Griffin*!"

The *Griffin* landed and started running at her, while the *Stinger* shifted left, pulling Harrigan toward them. Lisa flipped the safeties off her triggers. Her weapons—twin light PPCs and multiple missile launchers—were ready. She tapped a button loading large-range missiles into the launchers.

Both her *Gauntlet* and the opposing *Griffin* weighed the same, and had roughly the same sort of long-range firepower; The *Griffin* had the advantage of jump jets, while the *Gauntlet* had better short-range firepower. But the Republic 'Mech had to fire first.

A thousand meters separated them now, but that was closing as the two charged each other. "Foxtrot Six to all elements! Do not fire first if you can avoid it!"

By now, Charlie's APCs had raced past the Republic 'Mechs, moving too fast to be easily hit as they headed for the town. As they approached, a pair of Vedettes emerged from the cover of buildings. Immediately, all four Guards APCs twisted and angled away from the new threat. Lisa could see Republic soldiers running among the buildings.

The distance between her and the Republic *Griffin* had shrunk to less than six hundred meters. Lisa restrained the urge to trigger her MMLs, despite now being in range. Instead, she angled left, toward a stand of trees with green-blue leaves and wide, thick trunks. She triggered the MASC and her *Gauntlet* picked up even more speed, pushing a hundred kilometers an hour.

She was in fifty meters of the trees when there was an explosion from the town's direction, followed by intense gunfire.

"Hostile contact!" Boom-Boom shouted. "Enemy tank opened fire on us!"

"Get to the civilians and protect them!" Lisa shouted. "Delta Six, Foxtrot Six. Republic force is confirmed hostile!"

"Acknowledged. ETA sixty seconds."

The *Griffin* opened fire, its LRMs a twisting, writhing mass flying at Lisa. She triggered her MASC again, giving her an extra boost of speed at the right moment as the swarm of missiles slammed into the ground behind her, ripping up the soil in thick, black chunks.

Her reply of LRMs exploded from her launchers, sending nearly as many missiles back at the *Griffin*. The Republic 'Mech darted right, avoiding all but a couple of missiles, which struck its left leg.

First blood to me, Lisa thought.

She angled away from the trees, running behind them instead of into them. She charged around the grove at a full run, bring her targeting reticle onto the *Griffin* once again. She could hear Hannigan's rotary autocannon spitting out a long burst of rounds, but her attention was on the *Griffin*.

Another volley of LRMs flew from her MMLs just as the *Griffin* fired its own LRMs. The two swarms flew at each other, several exploding as they crossed each other's flights, the survivors zoomed on. Lisa jerked left, but several missiles struck her right arm and torso. She rode out the hits and then darted right, keeping her *Gauntlet* facing the *Griffin*. The Republic 'Mech was moving to Lisa's right, and now brought its particle projection cannon into the fight. The crackling blue beam struck a couple of meters behind the *Gauntlet*, leaving a meter-deep trench in the ground.

Lisa waited until she heard the next load of LRMs feed into the launchers, She fired them as well as both light PPCs. One beam smashed into the *Griffin's* left hip, while the other one scarred the ground near the Republic 'Mech's foot. The LRMs did a little better, about half of them peppering the *Griffin's* torso. The 'Mech rode out the attack, but it was enough to allow Lisa to close the difference.

The *Griffin* began backpedaling, trying to keep its distance. Lisa changed missile magazines, loading SRMs into the *Gauntlet's* MMLs, then using her MASC to close on the 'Mech. When she got within a hundred and eighty meters, she fired, sending over a dozen short-range missiles at the *Griffin*. The Republic 'Mech staggered as most of the missile swarm smashed into its torso and arms. One of Lisa's light PPC blasts passed over the *Griffin's* shoulder, while the second blast cracked armor on the medium 'Mech's left leg.

"Foxtrot Six! Clear the area!" She recognized McWalsh's voice and immediately changed direction, breaking off her attack. As she moved away, her sensors picked up an incoming flights of missiles from behind her.

The *Griffin* had only a few seconds to react before another score of missiles struck it, staggering it even more. The Republic pilot regained their balance, but the combination of missiles and energy impacts left the *Griffin* battered. It turned toward Lisa, its PPC coming up, only to stagger again as a blazing blue energy bolt slammed into its side.

"Attention, Republic forces!" McWalsh said over the radio, his voice stern. "Surrender now!"

The *Griffin* launched into the air, away from both Lisa and the advancing armor. It landed nearer the town and behind it, Lisa saw several APCs move. She loaded LRMs again and looked around. All four of her lance were still standing, as were all four

Republic 'Mechs, though they looked worse for wear and had fallen back toward the town.

Lisa heard the rumble of approaching armor, and saw a Guards Manticore II come into view. Farther away, she could see the rest of Delta Able roll into view, with the mechanized infantry of Delta Bravo APCs behind them.

"This isn't over yet, intruder!" Major Plenosi growled.

"You want round two, come on," McWalsh replied coolly. "I've already called for reinforcements, and there's a squadron of aerospace fighters that'll be here in five minutes and additional ground forces in ten."

More Republic military vehicles were moving out of the town, turning south and moving away at a high rate of speed. Lisa changed channels. "Boom-Boom! Status?"

"We're holed up in the church with several hundred civs!" the battle armor leader replied, talking fast. "Several of our suits have been dinged, but we're all right!"

"What's happening in the town?"

"Reps are heading for the hills! They're clearing out as fast as they can!"

"Stay there until we come in and clear the area!"

The last Republic vehicles left the town, and the 'Mech lance began pulling back to cover them. "Delta Six to all mobile Delta elements." McWalsh's tone was cautious, but commanding. "Advance slowly toward the town. Do not fire unless you're fired on. If they want to leave, we will not stop them."

The *Kampfgruppe* move forward at a walk, and the Republic 'Mechs fell back slowly, shielding the rest of their comrades. After several tense minutes, the *Kampfgruppe* was north of the town, the Republic south. As soon as McWalsh's unit reached the town itself, the Republic *Commando* and *Arctic Fox* turned and ran after the rest of the unit. After twenty seconds passed, the *Griffin* and *Stinger* launched themselves into the air on plumes of plasma. Twisting in midair, they landed with their backs to the town and raced away.

"Foxtrot, form a picket line south of town," McWalsh said. "Bravo, I need you to sweep the town for any injured civvies and surprises left behind by the Reps. Echo, follow the Reps and see where they're going and make sure they're not doubling back. Charlie, check the civs and see if they need any first aid and find me the town leaders. Reinforcements will be here in a few minutes. Let's get busy people."

CHAPTER 19

EUROPA
JAHRESZEITWUNDER
MELISSIA
JADE FALCON OCCUPATION ZONE
25 FEBRUARY 3151

Chard Schumacher considered himself a patriot.

Established inside Europa, Schumacher was one of the few Republic agents operating within the enemy's capital. His coffee bar, near the Council headquarters, made it a perfect place to pick up bits of intelligence he could pass on to his Republic contact.

Nearing forty, he didn't look like a spy. He was balding, a few kilos overweight, and a face that was too long and broad to be attractive. He was a bachelor with no close family and no close friends. His coffee bar—and spy work—was his life.

He had just closed the bar for the night when the phone rang. He was alone, the rest of his night staff having left for the evening. Sighing, he picked up the phone. "Schumacher's Coffee Bar."

"We must be one with the light," a voice said.

Schumacher's face slackened. "One with the light," he muttered.

"Listen carefully," the voice said. "We have chosen you for an important mission."

"Important mission," Schumacher intoned.

He listened to the instructions for several minutes, repeating key information as the voice instructed him on his mission. Finally, he put the receiver back into its cradle and the slack face was replaced with a large smile. He had a mission!

He finished cleaning up and went up to his apartment about the coffee bar. He went to the closet and took out a long case. He opened it and smiled down at the Praetorian S-5 rifle nestled inside the case. He ran his hand over the weapon. He had to make sure it was ready to fire, and that would take some time. Then bed, and getting up early to start his mission.

It was good to be doing something for the Republic!

Pocasio folded the perscomm and handed it to the man sitting next to him, who slipped it into his pocket. Before morning, the unit would be disassembled, and the parts scattered in a dozen dumpsters across the city.

They were sitting in a van, half a block down from Schumacher's Coffee Bar. Pocasio and the man were sitting in front, with two more men sitting behind them. They were all dressed in dark clothing, and if anyone approached them, they were also armed.

"I don't like this," the second man said. He had a bullet-shaped head and was bald. "He's one of our best sleepers."

"It's necessary," Pocasio growled. "He's the only one in a position to possibly know about Brewer's arrival tomorrow."

"He isn't a trained sniper."

"He'll do well enough."

"And if he misses?"

"That's why you and your team will move in after Schumacher leaves and plant the items in the back. Make them hard to find, but not too hard. We want this to point directly at the Republic."

"I know my job," the man growled.

"See that you do."

A car rolled up next to the van. Pocasio got out and said, "Call me when you're done."

"Of course."

Pocasio got into the back of the car. The driver said, "Where to?"

"My office," Pocasio growled. "I have work to do."

CHAPTER 20

EUROPA
JAHRESZEITWUNDER
MELISSIA
JADE FALCON OCCUPATION ZONE
28 FEBRUARY 3151

Vedet Brewer felt the *Blade's Edge* land on the DropPort's tarmac and closed his eyes. The last three days had been unpleasant in the aftermath of the Gildfield Gap incident. The Republic had been angry, and Vedet had spent much of his time speaking to Mendez via video from the *Evening Star.* Part of him wanted to go down to the Rock, but Mendez advised him not to, citing "unrest by the rank and file." Vedet had released the videos Delta had recorded in and round Gildfield Gap to both the Republic and the media. The broadcast had sent the Republic into a frenzy, the minority parties in parliament demanding answers from the Prime Minister and the Freedom Party. That had added another reason to avoid the Rock for now.

He leaned back and wished he could spend more time with Callisto. They tried to get a few minutes alone every time he went to the Rock, but even then, it was limited to a few quiet sentences with each other before they had to separate and go about their business. The comparison of the DNA samples had to wait until the *Evening Star* was on-planet, as the procedure required gravity and time.

Since going into the Republic was out, that left the Council to visit. He had turned down the graf's invitation to his estate, deciding it was too much of a risk.

The DropShip came to a stop. There was a *beep*, and the *Edge*'s captain said, "We have landed. Clear the bays for vehicle deployment."

Vedet yawned and looked at his watch. It would take a few minutes to unload the vehicles and deploy them. He hated the waiting, but it also gave him a couple of minutes to get his "game face" on.

"Not the most fun place I've seen," said a male voice.

Vedet turned and looked in the speaker's direction, on the new "military aides" assigned to him. Hans Muller was a tall, broadly built man with thick features and short, blond hair. He was dressed in a MechWarrior's coveralls, and a gun belt was hanging over the edge of his chair.

The MechWarrior sitting across from him, a short, petite woman with sharp features, sighed. "Hans?"

"*Ja*, Hauptmann?"

"Shut up and get ready. Cowboy!"

The tall, lean man sitting behind the hauptmann had a Stetson pulled down over his face. At her yell, he moved languidly, pushing up his hat's brim, revealing a weatherbeaten face of all sharp angles and clear blue eyes. "No need to yell, Viv," he drawled. "I'm sleeping, not deaf."

Vivian Neece, Echo Company's CO, twisted around in her chair to look at Cowboy. "It's Showtime, Lee, so wake up and get ready."

"I'm awake," Lee Goode replied, stretching slowly.

Neece looked over at Vedet and saw him looking at her. "Sorry, Your Grace," she said, her cheeks coloring with embarrassment. "Muller and Goode are better behaved."

"I'm familiar with Echo company's reputation," Vedet said mildly. "Just stay with me and keep your eyes open."

"Roger that, Your Grace," Goode said rising to his feet. "We won't embarrass you."

Bronislaw rose to his feet as the shuttle slowed to a stop. "Hauptmann," he said to Neece. "You and Muller will be first out and wait for us at the foot of the stairs. The Duke will be out next, then myself, and finally Goode. Once we are on the ground, Reverse triangle formation, Muller and Goode out front, the Duke and myself in the middle, and the Hauptmann behind me. Keep your eyes open and look for anything out of the ordinary."

"Got it, Hoss," Godde said. Bronislaw shot him a stony look, then headed for the hatch.

As Vedet rose to his feet, he wondered if the graf would offer anything new.

In the shadow of an exhaust fan on top of a DropPort warehouse, Schumacher gazed at the *Fury*-class DropShip that had landed, and he smiled. His target was here!

He took the Praetorian S-5 from its case and stared through the sight at the DropShip, gaging the distance. The sniper rifle's sight was designed to help him calculate the range and wind.

Once the rangefinder reported the DropShip was 753 meters away, he relaxed and waited.

By the time Vedet reached the hatchway, both Neece and Muller were heading down the stairs. Bronislaw stepped out first, scanning the area for any obvious threats. Seeing none, he stepped back, allowing Vedet to pass him and start down the stairs.

The air was dry and warm, and there were only a few clouds in the sky. It looked like it was going to be a good day.

On the warehouse, Schumacher hesitated when the woman appeared at the hatchway. She started down the stairs, followed by a man who wasn't his target.

"No," he muttered. "Not the target."

A giant appeared at the hatchway and scanned the area. Schumacher felt a chill go through him as he watched the giant.

His briefing package said this giant was the target's bodyguard. If he was here, then—

He saw someone moved past the giant and start down the stairs. He followed the new person and smiled as he saw it was his target. He centered the Praetorian's sights on the target and let the scope do the calculations. After several seconds there was a soft *beep* and the scope showed the target solution.

Steadying his aim, Schumacher tightened his finger on the trigger...

Vedet's right foot was just touching the tenth step when something fast and hard slammed into his right shoulder, sending him into the left-hand rail of the stairs. Pain roared along his right side, and he couldn't think of anything else.

His knees weakened, and he started falling forward. Suddenly, he was grabbed by the back of the collar and pulled up the stairs and back into the DropShip. As soon as he was back inside, his vision went dark.

Bronislaw thrust the Duke's body into Goode's arms "Sickbay, now!" he roared at Cowboy. "Then get the *Blade* into the air as soon as the hatch is closed!" He spun back to the hatchway, and charged out, a large pistol appearing in his hand. "Bronislaw here!" he shouted into the radio. "Ground forces, deploy smoke now!"

By the time he hit the third step down, wisps of smoke were in the air. He glanced to his right, toward where the shot that had come from. He saw a couple warehouses in that direction. "Hesperus Guards!" he roared, pointing in that direction with his free hand. "The shot came from over there!"

By the time his feet hit the tarmac, thick, white smoke was everywhere. Neece and Muller were waiting for him, pistols out. "Follow me!" he roared as he spun and charged toward a Saxon APC that had been unloaded from the *Blade's Edge*. He reached it just as the *Fury*'s engines began turning, filling the area with noise and making the smoke swirl.

He reached the APC and looked back at the two MechWarriors. "Get in!" he shouted.

Muller and Neece dove inside just as the door began closing, while Bronislaw grabbed the bar above the door and planted his feet on the skirt. He spotted the Saxon's ID number and shouted into his comm set. "Saxon Three, get us over to those warehouses *now!*"

After a moment, the Saxon started moving.

Schumacher panicked. He was certain he had hit his target, but the giant had carried him out of view before he could fire again. Then that had been followed by smoke and the DropShip had started its engines. He had to be sure!

He swung the S-5 toward the DropShip's cockpit. Maybe if he put enough rounds into the cockpit, he could prevent the target from escaping. He growled in frustration as smoke covered the DropShip's nose and cockpit. He fired anyway, sending a half dozen rounds into the smoke in the general area where he thought the cockpit was.

He was firing the sixth round when movement caught his attention. He saw several APCs fly out of the smoke, heading toward him. Time to go!

He dropped the rifle back into the case, closed it, and started running across the roof to the access ladder he'd used to get up here. They couldn't know exactly where the shot had come from. If he could get to his car, he could still escape!

The case had a sling, so he slung it over his back and started down the ladder.

The Saxon came to a stop between two of the warehouses. Bronislaw released his hold and stepped back as the doors opened and Muller and Neece, along with a platoon of soldiers leaped out. "Search these warehouses!" the Elemental ordered. He motioned at both Muller and Neece. "You two, with me!"

As the troops scattered, two more Saxons came to a stop and discharged their infantry. An officer ran over to Bronislaw. "What happened?"

"Sniper," Bronislaw replied, holstering his pistol and reaching into the Saxon and removing a support machine gun from its cradle with one hand, grabbing several large drums of ammo with the other. "They shot the duke, and I don't know how badly he was hit. The sniper is somewhere around here. Find and detain anyone. Do not kill anyone unless there is no other choice." He slotted a drum magazine into the machine gun and yanked the bolt back. "Let us go hunting."

Schumacher was three-quarters of the way down the ladder when he heard shouts and people running. He increased speed, his arms and legs burning from the effort. When he hit the ground, he began running. His car was only a couple of hundred meters away. If he could get to it—

"Hey, you!"

Still running, he glanced back and saw a couple of soldiers in field uniforms standing at the corner of the warehouse he had just descended from. Growling, he drew a pistol from his belt and fired blindly behind him, wincing at the loudness of the pistol shots. He heard curses and shouts, but kept running. He still had a ways to go.

The pistol shots made Bronislaw's head turn in that direction. "We've got a runner!" a soldier shouted over the radio. "Middle-aged, pudgy, carrying a big case on his back and has a pistol. He just shot at us!"

"This is Bronislaw," the Elemental growled into the radio. "Where?"

"Behind warehouse fourteen and running past warehouse fifteen!"

"Hauptmann!" Bronislaw said. "Two squads with me, Neece and Muller. You take two squads and directly pursue. I will see if I can cut him off. We need him alive."

"Yes, sir!" the officer shouted. "Squads one and three with me! Squads two and four with the bodyguards! Move."

Bronislaw didn't wait, but turned and ran down the line of warehouses, followed by the two squads and the two MechWarriors.

Schumacher's legs felt like they'd been dipped in acid and his lungs felt as if he'd inhaled hot coals. He was halfway to his car now, but he heard his pursuers getting closer. He pointed the pistol back over his shoulder, but when he pulled the trigger, all he heard was the hammer falling on an empty chamber. Snarling in frustration, he flung the pistol behind him.

He altered his path to skirt around several cargo pallets. He passed several of them, losing sight of his pursuers. He was running on willpower alone, and his heart was in his throat. He only had another seventy-five meters to—

As he passed another cargo pallet stack, something reached out and grabbed him. His feet went out from under him, and he was suddenly airborne. Then the same something slammed him into the ferrocrete hard enough to take his breath away and stun him.

By the time his eyes refocused, all he could see was a large muzzle several millimeters away pointed between his eyes. He looked past the muzzle and saw the giant glaring down at him. "Surrender," the man growled.

"I think that's wise advice," a woman wearing a jumpsuit said. She was also pointing a weapon at Schumacher, but compared to the muzzle filling half his view, it could have been a water pistol.

Schumacher flopped around for a few seconds until the giant ground the muzzle between his eyes. "Don't move," the giant growled. Schumacher stopped moving.

The giant looked at the woman. "Get him up, restrain him, make sure he has no surprises on him, but do no physical harm to him. Put him into a Saxon with a squad and Muller." The giant stepped back, but the machine gun was still pointed at his head.

Schumacher felt himself picked up, the rifle case removed, and his arms bound behind him. The enemy soldiers around him were all giving him murderous looks, but he didn't care. He had hopefully completed his assignment.

Bronislaw watched the sniper hauled away, his expression dark and angry. The sound of a DropShip lifting off made him turn and watch the *Blade's Edge* lift into the air. He tapped his comm headset. "Bronislaw to *Blade's Edge*. We have the sniper. What is the duke's status?"

"He took a bullet to the shoulder," Goode replied "We're heading for Fillyra. Command has already been alerted, and General Kirk has already dispatched transport to pick you and the others up. ETA is eight hours."

"Acknowledged, *Blade's Edge*. Do not worry about us. The Duke is the only thing you need to concern yourself with."

CHAPTER 21

FILLYRA
JAHRESZEITWUNDER
MELISSIA
JADE FALCON OCCUPATION ZONE
28 FEBRUARY 3151

Vedet's eyes fluttered open, the bright light making him close them again before opening them again. His right shoulder ached, and he felt weak and tired.

A face appeared over him. "Your Grace," the person said. It took him a few seconds to recognize Dr. Constantine Ginley.

"How long?" he tried to say, but the words came out as unconnected sounds. Ginley vanished, and Vedet felt his upper body being raised. More of the room came into view, showing a typical hospital room. A soft hum made him turn his head and look at the large machine sitting next to his bed, showing his life signs. Goode was standing in a corner of the room, his hat down over his eyes.

Ginley appeared with a covered cup with a straw sticking out of it. "Drink, Your Grace." Vedet sucked greedily on the straw, and cold water flooded his mouth, soothing his dry throat and mouth.

"Right," Ginley said, "You're in Fillyra, at the Gold Star Hospital. Twelve hours ago, you were shot when you were coming down the DropShip's stairs. Bronislaw carried you back into the DropShip and ordered it to lift off. He then led your escort in running down and capturing the sniper. They're on their way here now, and should be here shortly."

"How bad?" Vedet rasped.

"How bad are you wounded? Considering the circumstances, you're lucky to be alive. Ten centimeters lower and to the left, and it would have shattered your sternum, even with your bulletproof vest. As it was, the bullet shattered your collarbone and just missed the shoulder socket, and when you hit the railing, you cracked a couple of ribs. We've cleared out the bone and bullet fragments, and I've already scheduled sessions to replace the missing bone fragments. I suggest you stay in bed for an entire week, but knowing you, that will most likely be an impossibility."

Ginley turned away. "There's several people waiting to see you, and the other members of Echo Company are camped outside the room since you arrived. As for the suspect, Bronislaw made sure the sniper is healthy for interrogation."

"Good. What about the graf?"

"The Council? By the time their security showed up, Bronislaw already had the location cleaned up and told them you'd suddenly taken ill and were being evaced to Fillyra. The graf sent his regrets, and hopes you feel better soon."

Vedet nodded, and groaned as the pain flared through his shoulder. Ginley sighed. "You are on bed rest for an absolute minimum of three days. It should be a week, but I'd have a better chance of being elected First Lord of the Star League than keeping you in bed that long."

Vedet snorted. "Do you always have this smooth a bedside manner?"

"Only with my important patients." He glanced at his watch. "I'll let Midori and Thomas know you're awake."

Twenty minutes later, both Thomas Kirk and Midori Jennings were standing in Vedet's hospital room. After expressing their pleasure at seeing their duke still alive, they got down to business.

"Let's start with the military situation," Vedet said. He was sitting up at a forty-five-degree angle. Vivian Neece was standing in a corner of the room, a submachine gun slung over one shoulder. "Has there been any change in either side's movements or actions?"

Kirk shook his head. "Nothing that would indicate they're trying to take advantage of your...condition. There have been a few run-ins in the field, but both sides have backed off before anyone started shooting. There have been reports of a Council offense brewing against both Grizano and Zarko. If they take them, the Council will control the entire Broad Run River Valley and most of the farmland on the planet."

"What do our sources say?"

"Additional troops are being moved into position to attack both towns, butthey're mostly troops belonging to other members of the Council, with only a handful of mercenary BattleMechs to stiffen them."

"That's interesting," Vedet muttered. "He's holding back."

"Yes, Your Grace," Jennings replied. "The question is why?"

"Speculate."

"Laskaris wants his forces for a big strike."

"The Rock," Kirk said.

Jennings nodded. "A reasonable assumption."

"Look into that more, Midori. If that's his plan, let's know that now then later."

"Yes, Your Grace."

"Now, let's get back to the elephant in the room—my would-be assassin."

"The suspect, along with Bronislaw and the others, arrived fifteen minutes ago. We have identified him as Chard Schumacher, a coffee bar owner. He's forty-three, no military experience, has never been off Melissia."

"Doesn't quite fit the profile of an assassin."

"No, he doesn't. After we established his identity, I sent Bale and Ramsey to his apartment to locate any evidence. The Council security forces had already blocked off the street and were searching the building."

"Which makes you wonder how they found out about him, doesn't it?" Kirk asked.

"Yes, it does," Vedet replied. "Do whatever you have to, Midori. I want to know why Schumacher tried to kill me."

"Rest assured, Your Grace. My people are very good at getting people to talk."

Vedet looked over at Kirk. "I take it security is tight?"

"The entire floor is ours, and we have two-person teams on every floor. The only people allowed in here are six members of Guards medical staff, Dr. Ginley, Bronislaw, Echo Company, and Midori and myself. If an assassin got as far as this floor, Bronislaw is outside the door carrying a support machine gun, and Echo Company's sleeping in the break room next door. Outside the hospital, *Kampfgruppe* Delta is handling perimeter security. The hospital isn't happy about our precautions, but they'll put up with us for a few days."

"I intend on spending as little time as possible in this bed," Vedet said. "I don't enjoy being an immobile target any more than you do."

"For now, that bed is where you'll be," Kirk said.

Vedet nodded. "I know, but I need to keep on top of things and communicate with both sides."

The two men glanced at each other, then Jennings looked back to Vedet. "We expected you'd feel this way, so I've secured equipment and put together an overview of the last couple of days."

"Well, bring it all in," Vedet said with a pained smile. "At least you know I can't walk out on your briefings."

CHAPTER 22

Due to his injuries, Vedet found himself limited in what he could do. They kept him updated on what the Guards were doing and what both sides of the war were up to. The Council had claimed both Grizano and Zarko from the Republic in bitter fighting, taking the entire river valley and most of the planet's farmable lands.

The next target appeared to be the city of Gorath, which controlled several important roads and railway lines. Taking Gorath would cripple the Republic's ability to quickly shift forces north and south, and leave the Rock open to an assault. Both sides were building forces to either take or defend the city—Council mercenary BattleMechs were aggressively patrolling between the valley and Gorath, while the Republic was moving forces into Gorath and turning it into a fortress. Both sides were avoiding Hesperus Guards patrols, but there had been several clashes between the two warring sides.

As for the population, the Duke and his Guards were rapidly becoming the alternative to both the Council and the Republic. Polls in both Council and Republic territory had Vedet leading, and a few people were calling for him to become the leader of a new world government. The Hesperus troops, wherever they patrolled, were treated as heroes and liberators. The calls were making people in both capitals nervous.

With great reluctance, Ginley allowed Vedet to sit in a chair while he worked. It made things a little easier, and helped hide his weakness when he talked to the leaders on both sides. As far as they were concerned, Vedet had been hit hard with a local variant of influenza, but was recovering. Neither side was willing to meet with the other, and both sides were still trying to recruit him and his Guards to their side.

After a morning of briefings and conversations with senior members of both sides, Vedet was tired and ready for a nap. He was getting ready to call for help to move back to the bed when the door opened and Jennings stepped inside. "Your Grace?"

"What is it?" Vedet asked, irritated.

"Miss Mylonasa and Colonel Nathanson are here."

"What?"

Jennings nodded. "Do you wish to see them?"

The DNA tests he'd ordered had finally been completed. Vedet had taken the news with little emotion. As of now, only three people knew the results; himself, Jennings, and the medical technician who had done the test, and the technician was unaware of the identities of the DNA samples.

Vedet exhaled, touched the ring he was wearing under his shirt, then nodded. Jennings stepped out of the room and was back a few seconds later, with Callisto and Nathanson, trailed by Bronislaw. Vedet noticed they were holding hands in a way that sought comfort from the other.

Callisto gasped when she saw him sitting there. "Are you all right?" she asked, the words tumbling out of her mouth in a rush.

"I'm fine."

"How badly were you shot?" Nathanson asked.

Vedet frowned at him. "What makes you think I was shot?"

He motioned at the sling on Vedet's right arm. "I don't know many bouts of Desian Flu that need slings."

"I'll live. What are you doing here?"

"The prime minister sent us. Rumors are floating around that you're dead, and a computer-generated imposter has been dealing with the Prime Minister and his cabinet for the last couple of sessions. The Freedom Party is pushing for declaring the Hesperus Guards as invaders and to order Republic forces be issued a 'kill on sight' orders."

Vedet leaned back in his chair and sighed. "Idiots," he muttered.

"That may be," Nathanson said. "The Prime Minister is delaying things to give us time to come out and talk to you in person."

"Well, you can report I am alive and recovering."

"What happened?" Callisto asked.

"As the colonel has surmised, I was shot."

"By who?"

Vedet was silent for a moment. Chard Schumacher's interrogation had been, in Jennings words, "problematic." While Schumacher claimed to be a Republic agent, Jennings' people, experts in interrogation, had found signs that someone with skills far beyond either side's known technical ability had mentally conditioned him. There were still too many questions, and Vedet wasn't ready to let word get out. "We're not sure yet."

Just then, Jennings entered. "Your Grace, Graf Laskaris is here with Baron Pocasio. They just crossed the outer perimeter and should be inside the hospital in three minutes."

Callisto expression was torn between fear and anger. "He can't find us here!"

"He won't," Vedet said firmly. "Midori, escort these two to an empty room on this floor. Then get down to the main entrance and escort the graf and baron up here."

"Yes, Your Grace."

Nathanson glared at Vedet. "You've been talking to them, haven't you?"

"I've been listening to both sides," the duke replied. "We can discuss the rest later. I'm sure neither one of you want to run into the graf."

After shooting Vedet an ugly look, Nathanson escorted Callisto out of the room. Vedet motioned for Bronislaw to come over. "Get this damned sling off me and stand behind me while our guests are here. Watch both of them carefully, especially Pocasio."

Several minutes later, Jennings led Graf Laskaris and Baron Pocasio into the room. "Duke Brewer," Laskaris said with a wide smile. "I see you are doing well."

"I've been better."

Laskaris' smile faded, and he looked back at Jennings, who was standing near the door then at Bronislaw, who was standing behind the duke's chair. "May we speak as nobles and men?"

"Mr. Jennings and Bronislaw enjoy my full confidence. Whatever you need to say can be said in front of them."

"Very well." Laskaris shot a look at Pocasio, who didn't change expression, then looked back at Vedet. "I found out this morning that someone tried to assassinate you two days ago."

"Oh?" Vedet replied.

"Is it true?"

"It is. I was lucky. I must compliment you on your sources."

"My sources are very good."

"That puts you ahead of the Republic."

"Oh, I'm sure they're well-aware of their failure. They'll pay for it and the other crimes they've committed in the name of that so-called *Republic*!"

"We want to speak about the suspect," Pocasio said.

"As far as I know, he got away," Vedet said. "Have you identified him?"

"We believe he's Chard Schumacher, a man we've suspected of being a Republic spy for some time."

"Oh? Have you found him?"

"No, we think he's gone to ground."

"Well, I'll make sure my security people are on alert for him."

Laskaris glanced around and spotted a high-backed wooden chair in the room's corner. "May I sit?"

"Please do."

The graf walked over, picked up the chair, and placed it in front of Vedet. He sat, Pocasio stepping up behind him. "I think we've been beating around the bush long enough, Duke Brewer. I think you realize by now the Republic thinks you're nothing more than an interloper—this assassination attempt proves that. They're a dying state, and won't last more than six months. Allying with them is a losing proposition. Even now, we're moving forces to seize Gorath from them."

Vedet rested his elbows on the chair's armrests and steepled his fingers in front of him, steeling his face so he didn't show any discomfort from his still healing injury. "What are you offering?"

"Besides being on the winning side?" Laskaris smiled. "How about reducing casualties? With your Guards working alongside my forces, we can win the war quickly and stop the bloodshed."

Vedet nodded slowly. "We could, but I'm going to need more than that. If we side with you, we're going to lose a lot of the goodwill we've built up in our time here."

Laskaris smiled. "I could help you regain the Archon's throne."

Vedet raised an eyebrow. "Tharkad is a long way from here."

"I have powerful friends who would be a great help. They know Trillian is weak, and the Commonwealth needs a strong leader."

"Your friends on Medellin?"

Laskaris's smiled dimmed slightly before returning to its former brightness. "Among others. They can supply money and equipment for any size army you need. No, the friends I'm talking about are nobles like yourself, those who have influence at the court at Tharkad, in the Estates General, and elsewhere in the Commonwealth. I have many favors I can call in, and I'm willing to do that for you, in return for your help."

Vedet nodded slowly, his expression considering what the graf had said. "Powerful friends, huh?"

Laskaris spread his hands wide. "Of course. One can never have enough of them."

"That's true. I could use powerful friends." Vedet smiled. "I will consider your offer. I will be here for a few more days, then spend the rest of week at the Fillyra Continental resting and getting some physical therapy. I'll let you know my decision before the week is out."

"Excellent!" Laskaris shot to his feet. "I await your answer. Until then, rest and get well soon. Good day, Duke." He turned and headed for the door. Pocasio was two steps ahead of the graf and opened the door. Laskaris walked out of the room, followed by the baron. The door closed behind them, leaving Jennings, Bronislaw, and Vedet alone in the room.

Before Vedet could say anything, Bronislaw placed a hand over his employer's mouth and held a finger to his lips. He then looked at Jennings. "Is it not time for the Duke's physical therapy session?"

Jennings' expression didn't change. "I believe you're right. I'll get a wheelchair. I'll be right back." The spymaster left the room at a quick walk.

Bronislaw removed his hand from Vedet's face, pointed to the wall, held up two fingers, and put his hand to his ear. "I will check on the security," he said, walking over to the chair Laskaris had used and picked it up.

"Before you go," Vedet said, "Help me get this sling back on."

"Yes, sir." Bronislaw ignored the order as he looked the chair over carefully. After a few seconds, he twisted the chair around so Vedet could see it, and pointed to a spot in the back of the chair under the backrest. Vedet leaned forward, grimacing at the pain and saw the small device, the size of his thumbnail, placed in one corner of the backrest. It was flat and had a woodgrain on it, making it difficult to be spotted easily.

Vedet nodded, and Bronislaw put the chair back where it had been. He took the sling out of his pocket and helped the duke put it into place. The groans Vedet made as he did so were genuine.

Ten minutes later, Vedet was sitting in a wheelchair in another hospital room on the floor. Across from him sat both Nathanson and Callisto, shown in by Jennings before leaving them with Muller and one of Echo Company's other MechWarriors, Jason Boyens, a short, powerfully built man with long sideburns.

Nathanson and Callisto sat close together on the bed, and Vedet noticed the pair holding hands. "How long have you two been a couple?"

The question startled both of them. It was Callisto who answered. "We've known each other since we were children. But we've only been romantically involved for three or four months."

"My Aunt Sophia rented a house from Callisto's grandparents," Nathanson added. "We played together until her grandparents died and she was sent to live with her mother."

"We're trying to keep it low-key," Callisto said. "Neither one of us is popular with the Freedom Party."

The door opened and Jennings entered, followed by Bronislaw. The Elemental looked at the two Echo members and nodded toward the door. Both MechWarriors took the hint and left, closing the door behind them.

"Well?" Vedet asked.

"We found a second listening device attached to your bed," Jennings said. "Sophisticated devices, not of local manufacture."

"Pocasio was subtle," Bronislaw said. "If I had not been watching him carefully, I would have missed him placing the devices."

Vedet nodded. "Good eye, Bronislaw. Midori, are the devices still in place?"

"Yes, Your Grace."

"Good. Leave them there. If we need to talk about important matters, we'll use this room, and use my room for items we want Pocasio to know about."

"Yes, Your Grace."

"What's going on?" Nathanson asked.

Vedet looked at the colonel. "The good graf offered me an alliance—in return for me helping him defeat the Republic, he would back me for the Archon's throne and have his off-world friends aid me with weapons, contacts, and money."

"And you believe him?" Callisto asked.

Vedet snorted, and winced in pain. "Of course not. Besides, being the Archon is only being trapped in a pit of vipers. Trillian can keep the throne, and I wish her luck, but that will not help Melissia. No, Melissia will have to stand on its own."

Out of the corner of his eye, he saw Jennings staring at his noteputer, then glanced up at the couple on the bed.

"What do you mean?" Nathanson said.

"I mean the Commonwealth will not be arriving anytime soon. If Melissia's going to survive, it's going to stand on its own. It's going to have to band together with other nearby planets and form its own alliance. When the day comes—if it comes—that the Commonwealth can reclaim these worlds, the citizens can vote whether they want to rejoin. But now, we have to band together and be ready to defend ourselves from the enemies that lurk out there."

"Under your rule?" Nathanson's suspicion was thick in his tone.

Vedet arched an eyebrow. "Would you prefer Laskaris in charge? No, I think the citizens are looking for new leadership, one that isn't tied to either Republic or Council."

"He's right," Callisto said. "Neither side is ready to be ruled by the other."

"Your Grace?" Jennings said.

Vedet waved him off, his attention on the couple. "The war has left both sides with deep wounds. I am the only person who can reach out to both sides. I've been listening, and my people have been working on a plan that will bring both sides together."

"Under your rule," Nathanson said again.

"If you can find someone else both sides will accept, I'm willing to step aside. Besides, I'm not intending on running the day-to-day affairs of Melissia."

"Your Grace?" Jennings said again.

"In a moment, Midori," Vedet said. "One thing I learned while I was Archon is that I can't micromanage multiple worlds. I needed trusted people who don't need me looking over their shoulder for every decision."

"Are you offering me a position?" Nathanson asked.

"Would you take one?"

"Your *Grace*!" Jennings barked.

Vedet looked at his spymaster. "What is it?"

"I know where the Toliver heir is."

"Oh. Are you sure?"

"Yes, Your Grace."

"Fine. Tell Thomas to get a team ready and—"

"*Your Grace!*" Midori yelled, startling Vedet. "There is no need to send *anyone* to get him. He's sitting on the bed with your daughter."

"*What?*" Vedet, staring at Jennings in shock.

"*What?*" Callisto said. "Daughter?"

Nathanson sighed. "What gave me away?"

"You're using your great-grandmother's maiden name, and the fact the only Mason Nathanson died at birth thirty-two years ago. It took some time to dig into the archives to find the data, and that's because I was looking for it."

"I see." Nathanson stood and bowed. "Your Grace, I am Matthew Toliver, Graf of Eastern Jahreszeitwunder."

Vedet nodded. "Your Grace."

"Can we disperse with the titles? I've spent most of my life without one, and I'm not ready to officially claim mine just yet."

"Very well, but know the woman sitting next to you is my daughter."

"How are you so sure?" Callisto asked.

Vedet smiled. "I ordered additional sets of DNA tests, and the results prove you are my daughter by blood."

Callisto sagged and closed her eyes. "I'd nursed the hope that you would come back one day and take me and Mother away. When Mother died, I lost that hope until you arrived. Part of me was scared you'd reject me, deny my existence."

Vedet took a deep breath. "Callisto, I've made many mistakes in my life. Loving your mother was the best decision I ever made, and the worst decision I ever made was not coming back to get her and you. That is something I live with every day and will continue to do so until the day I die."

Callisto stood and walked over to Vedet. He stood up slowly and held out his good arm. She slipped into his embrace, and Vedet grunted as she squeezed him. "Careful. Ribs are still tender."

She stifled a laugh, but loosened the hold. After several seconds, she released the hug and stepped back. "Thank you—Father."

He smiled and nodded at her. "You're welcome—Daughter." He looked over at Jennings. "Any other secrets we need to know about?"

"Not at the moment, Your Grace."

"What do we do now?" Toliver asked.

"Now, I recover from this wound, then we see what Laskaris is up to."

CHAPTER 23

EUROPA
JAHRESZEITWUNDER
MELISSIA
JADE FALCON OCCUPATION ZONE
4 MARCH 3151

Yiorgos looked up when Pocasio walked into his office. "What?"

"The latest from the devices," Pocasio replied. "They're discussing the plan we proposed for a combined strike at the Rock."

Laskaris smiled. "Good."

Pocasio scowled. "This is the last day Brewer is in the hospital. He's being moved to a secure suite in the Fillyra Continental. Brewer has a choice of several suites in the hotel, but has never mentioned which one. His soldiers have already secured the hotel, so it's going to be much more difficult to monitor their conversations there."

The graf leaned back and waved his hand. "No need. I think the assassination attempt helped push him toward us. Any signs of Schumacher?"

"No, and that concerns me. We chose him because he wasn't trained. He should have been easy to find. But he's vanished."

The graf scowled. "It is possible Brewer's people captured him?"

Pocasio nodded. "It's possible, but all he can tell them is he's a Republic spy."

"No chance he'll implicate us?"

"No. We made sure of that. They haven't mentioned Schumacher during any of their conversations."

"You sound frustrated, my friend," Laskaris said mildly. "Yes, Brewer escaped our assassination attempt, but it has pushed him into our camp almost by default. Let's be ready to take advantage of that."

"You're not...trusting him, are you?"

The graf leaned forward, his face darkening. "Of course I don't trust the bastard! He is a *tsakáli*—a jackal—looking to steal my glory!" He calmed himself with an effort and leaned back. "We are in an alliance of convenience, nothing more. We both know we can't trust the other long-term."

"So you're not going to support Brewer's claim to the Archon throne?"

"Why would I? I expect Brewer to be dead by the end of the battle."

Pocasio shook his head. "Don't discount his Guards. We only have Maldonado's goons and your *Fylakes* as a reserve force. Most of our field forces are tied up in the build-up to taking Gorath."

"I'll see if I can free up some forces from the assault on Gorath, just in case."

"How are you going to play this?"

Laskaris became serious. "If everything goes right, our combined forces will attack the Rock in four days. As you well know, no one is immune from war's whims. It is possible the good Duke will be killed in the heat of battle, just like Toliver was."

"You're assuming he's going to take the field? He's still recovering from a serious injury."

Laskaris laughed. "Of course he's going to take the field! Do you think he's going to allow his biggest trump card out of his grasp, even for a moment? No, he will take the field with his Hesperus Guards, to make sure they remain his and intact."

The baron narrowed his eyes. "You have a plan."

Laskaris smiled again, a cold, cruel smile. "I have a plan. Vedet Brewer will not survive the Battle of the Rock."

CHAPTER 24

Vedet guided his *Atlas III* down the ramp of the *Union*-Class DropShip. Around him, the rest of the Hesperus Guards were deploying from other DropShips and moving toward each unit's staging area.

The attack on the Rock was today. It had taken several days for both sides to iron out the details of how to plan the assault. Vedet let Kirk and Jennings do most of the planning as he rested to prepare for what was going to be a rough day for him. His shoulder and ribs were still sore, and while they were mostly healed, they were still weak, and riding around in a 100-ton war machine was not advisable under most circumstances.

But Vedet thought he had no choice. His troops needed him in the field, and he would not give Laskaris an advantage in their power struggle. He was going to be there, despite what his senior officers thought. It was as if he was a noble from two thousand years ago, leading his knights and men-at-arms into battle.

As he cleared the ramp, Vedet glanced over to see Bronislaw, in a suit of Elemental armor in Guard's colors, riding on his *Atlas'* shoulder like an armored parrot. The bodyguard hadn't been more than a dozen meters from him since the assassination attempt, so it wasn't a surprise that the man wanted to be on the battlefield with him. "Cannot be a bodyguard if I am stuck on the DropShip," he'd rumbled when asked.

He reached the bottom of the ramp, turned the 100-ton assault 'Mech to the right and moved to his own staging area. Echo Company was waiting for him. As his *Atlas III* approached them, he activated his radio and said, "Opinion of the terrain?"

"It's a dump," said Vivian Neece. Her *BattleMaster*-10S was a relic of the Jihad, but fully operational and ready to deal out punishment. "Rocks, rocks, and oh yeah—more rocks!"

"It's not too bad," another voice said. Vedet recognized it as Muller. His *Thanatos* was standing next to Neece. "There's more green here than where I grew up."

"Granted, not exactly a garden spot," Vedet said with a smile. Then in a more serious tone, he said, "You know your duties, and I promise I will not throw myself into battle unless it's absolutely necessary."

"With all due respect, Your Grace," Sergeant Jason Boyens said, "I'd sooner trust a Sea Fox merchant than these Council boys." His *Berserker* was a brawler, and Boyens liked to fight, both in and out of the cockpit.

"I agree with Boyens," Neece said.

"Monitor Laskaris," Vedet said firmly, "no matter what happens. Once things get going, it'll become chaotic quickly, so maintain your sectors at all times."

"And if they attack us, sir?" Sergeant Alister Wills asked. His *Götterdämmerung* was the second-lightest 'Mech in the unit, and its pilot the youngest.

"Your sole responsibility is protecting the Duke," Neece said.

"A moment, Hauptmann," Vedet said. "Sergeant Wills, if we are attacked, I intend on moving toward the nearest group of Hesperus Guards and rallying there. I don't intend on standing and fighting, and I don't expect you to do that, either. If we get into a fight, it will be a running one."

"Thank you, Your Grace," Wills said

"Don't thank me yet." He looked at the last two members of his guard. "Anything to add, Swanson, Goode?"

"No sir," Goode drawled. "Me and *Six-Gun Annie* are ready to defend God and your noble self." His *Marauder*-7R took a step back and half bowed.

"Goode, show some respect!" Codi Swanson hissed. Her *Crusader*-10S was a few meters left of the *Marauder*, and the 65-ton 'Mech's right leg was twitching as if wanting to kick the other Mech.

Vedet chuckled. "That's all right, Swanson," he said. "I expect that from soldiers, and I'll allow some latitude."

"I have nothing to add, Your Grace."

Vedet glanced at his cockpit chronometer. "We should move out soon. Hauptmann Neece, deploy your troops as you see fit."

"Yes, Your Grace."

The Guards moved toward the rendezvous point in a loose formation. Scouts, both vehicles and 'Mechs, ranged far ahead and to the flanks of the main body, looking for any ambushes. The armor, battle armor, and conventional infantry were on the flanks, with the armor leading.

Vedet was in the center of the formation with his guard. Kirk's regimental command company was in front of them, and two of the First's 'Mech companies in front of Kirk, while the other two 'Mech companies were behind Vedet as a rear guard.

Two hours into the march, Vedet switched his radio to a pre-selected channel. Once he had the green light showing the connection, he said, "Dagger to Sword. We are on the ground and Oscar Mike to the rendezvous. Everything ready?"

"We should be, Dagger," Toliver replied several seconds later.

The Republic was not happy when Callisto and Toliver had returned with the plan. The Freedom Party loyalists in the Cabinet had screamed loudly about it, threatening to take it to the public as an example of Mendez's incompetence. They thought the minority PM would back down in the face of the threat.

They were wrong.

Mendez had been working behind the scenes for several months, lining up support from the other minority parties and forming his own coalition. When the Freedom Party threatened to take the matter public and call for a new PM, Mendez had stood up in Parliament and asked for a vote of no confidence in his own government. The vote passed by a wide margin, leaving the Freedom Party flatfooted. Now, as a caretaker PM, Mendez immediately invoked the security laws the Freedom Party had rammed through early in their rule, and arrested every member who had threatened to make the plan public. Using the same laws, Mendez then invoked a security ban on any news articles that even reported the rumor of the plan.

With the political end of things taken care of, Mendez had moved quickly to bring the Republic military to his side. Freedom Party supporters were replaced with ones who were not, and internal security companies were redesignated as line infantry and sent to bolster the defenses at Gorath. Toliver was now the chief military aide to Mendez, and coordinating the Republic's response to the oncoming attack.

"Our ETA to the rendezvous point is two hours. We should be at the attack point three hours after that."

"Copy, Dagger. Good luck." There was a measure of silence, then Toliver said, "I'm heading out with the mobile force to intercept you. I will help distract Laskaris."

"How are you going to do that?"

"I'm piloting my uncle's *Thunder Hawk*. I plan to call him out before the battle."

Vedet was silent for a few seconds and touched Cassandra's ring he wore under his cooling vest. "One other thing, Sword."

"Yes?"

"We'll be having a talk later, about a certain lady we both know."

There was silence on Toliver's side for a few seconds before he replied, "I look forward to it, Dagger."

CHAPTER 25

Vedet's force arrived at the rendezvous point an hour later than he'd estimated.

Laskaris' forces were already there, waiting for them. Vedet's eyes narrowed as he saw over three battalions of Council 'Mechs waiting for them. "Someone's been hiding things," he said on the channel he shared with the First's command lance.

"Yes sir," Kirk replied from his *Fafnir*'s cockpit. "Midori says the satellites are tracking more Council 'Mechs right now. Two more Council 'Mech companies around Gorath, and another company stationed at Europa. We're looking at better than four 'Mech battalions."

"Where did he hide them all?" Goreson asked. Her *Sunder*'s arms were twitching, reflecting her impatience.

"I don't know," Vedet said. "Thomas, get Midori's people to identify the merc leaders and find any fault lines. Have you spotted Laskaris yet?"

"*Titan II* on the hill to our right, five hundred meters."

"Maldonado?"

"The *Emperor* standing next to Laskaris."

Vedet looked in that direction and saw the graf's 'Mech standing on the hill with several others in Republic colors of blue and red. The mercenary colonel's *Emperor* was standing a few meters away, pained in similar colors like the Fylakes, but in a different scheme. Around the base of the hill, a cordon of vehicles and infantry—a battalion of Laskaris' *Fylakes*—were set up, keeping everyone away from their leader.

"Helen, get a feel for Laskaris' force," Vedet said as he headed for the graf's position. His guard moved with him, staying close and acting as a mobile shield. Vedet's *Atlas III* stopped by the Fylakes' cordon, letting his 'Mech loom over the armor and APCs. A few of the soldiers stepped back and Vedet saw some of them shaking in fear as they looked up at him.

The graf's *Titan II* turned toward them. "Well, well," Laskaris said over the radio, sounding cheerful as ever. "Aren't you a sight for sore eyes, Duke Brewer. I was thinking you weren't coming."

"Not to worry, my good graf," Vedet replied in the same cheerful tone. "We had to put down on the flatlands and hike over five hours to get here. The LAAF made damn sure assaulting this place wouldn't be easy."

Laskaris snorted. "You're telling me! Five times we hit this bunker—never made a dent. The old minefields are long gone, but the Republic rabble has some artillery rigged in the roof mounts, and they have every *damn* meter of ground plotted, with no cover."

"Just leave that to my aerospace wing," Vedet said. "Laser-guided bombs will take out the Long Toms, and then we can move in, kick their gates down, and crown you Landgrave of Melissia."

"Exactly. And then you get my support, and that of my network in the Commonwealth, to reclaim the Archonship on Tharkad. A fair exchange, I think."

An exchange, Vedet thought. *But how fair is it, really? Assuming I somehow survive the battle, how long would it be before I had an "accident"?*

Vedet paused as if he was looking around. "You have more forces here than I expected."

"The 'Mechs are on loan from my Medellin backers. Colonel Maldonado's mercenaries are very good with the knife work, but they're not the types you'd want to let loose around polite society. I've been holding them as my special reserve for keeping the barons in line."

"Very good, Graf. The Rock awaits. Let us begin our advance."

Fifteen minutes later, the combined force was clear of the foothills and advancing through the wide open space that surrounded the Rock. The mercenaries were leading the way, front and center, followed by the combined noble forces, mostly armor and infantry with a scattering of 'Mechs on the right flank.

The First Hesperus was on the left flank, a strong scouting/skirmishing line of hovertanks on its flank. A battalion of heavy armor was followed by a medium armor battalion, then the Guards' 'Mech battalion. The rest of the armor vehicles, battle armor, and infantry followed.

Behind them were Laskaris' *Fylakes*, and behind them, Laskaris, Vedet, and their personal guards. The rear guard comprised a mixed battalion of armor and 'Mechs.

The mercenaries, the noble forces, and the First will absorb most of the Republic's firepower, Vedet thought as he watched the force move forward. *Win or lose, Laskaris is planning to have the most intact force left on-planet when this is over.*

"Bad news is we're outnumbered three to one in 'Mechs," Goreson said over a private comm channel. "Good news is their numbers are skewed toward lights and mediums, with only a few heavies and assaults. We also have a slight advantage in technology. The barons have three mechanized infantry regiments, an armor demi-battalion, and two companies each of 'Mechs and battle armor. The *Fylakes* units comprise an armor regiment, a battle armor battalion, and four mechanized infantry regiments, leaning toward the light and medium end of the scale."

"They still have the numbers," Kirk said. "They'll quickly overwhelm us."

"If we allow them to," Vedet said. "When the time comes, myself and Echo Company will turn and hit Laskaris. The armor and battle armor will keep the *Fylakes* busy. The rest of the First will hold the line and keep the mercs off us. If Toliver has any luck, his force will hit the mercs while they're turning back toward us."

"What about the barons?" Goreson asked.

"Midori has a message ready to go when the fighting starts, but Toliver will speak to them first."

Vedet continued watching the mercenaries, and saw them become less and less cohesive, clumping up around their immediate superiors. *Definitely not disciplined. Either lack of training, or they haven't been on-planet that long, or both.*

Vedet picked out Laskaris' *Titan II*, five hundred meters to his left and another five hundred in front of him. After the initial conversation, the two senior nobles hadn't spoken directly to each other. Instead, one of Laskaris' subordinates had directed Vedet's and his Guards to move to the left flank.

He glanced at a side monitor, showing the land ahead. Laskaris was not overstating his claim of flat, clear ground around the Rock. There were several broken ridges between here and the fortress, but otherwise, anything taller than two meters tall was going to be visible from a long way away.

We'll be within the Rock's artillery range in less than five minutes, Vedet thought. *Not much time.* He tapped the radio channel between him and the Republic. "Dagger to Sword. We're on approach, five minutes out."

"Copy, Dagger," Toliver said. "We're Oscar Mike, ETA four minutes."

"Dagger." He switched channels. "Ready, Thomas?"

"Orders, Your Grace?" Kirk asked.

"We wait for Toliver to make his move first, then we go on my command. Once the fight starts, have our infantry designate the Graf's forces for the Rock's gunners so we can keep friendly fire to a minimum. With luck, putting Laskaris' and his people down quickly will make the other nobles hesitate."

They continued forward, Kirk slowly shifting his forces to be ready for the strike. After three minutes, someone shouted on a general channel, "Contact!"

Vedet stiffened in his chair.

"Direction and numbers!" Kirk barked.

"Checkpoint Buffalo!" the Hesperus Guards scout replied. Vedet glanced quickly at the map screen and saw it was only three kilometers in front of them. "We're looking at two-plus lances of 'Mechs and two companies of vehicles! Republic colors!"

Vedet saw a 'Mech appear on top of the ridge. His warbook spat out an ID: *Thunder Hawk*. The 100-ton 'Mech stood there and spread its arms wide.

"Attention council forces!" a new voice boomed across the shared channel. "I am Graf Matthew Toliver. Graf Yiorgos Laskaris, you are a murderer."

"Imposter!" Laskaris snarled.

"You are a liar, Yiorgos," Toliver continued in a disdainful tone. "You murdered my uncle and made it look like the Falcons did it. You seized my family's lands under the disguise of protection, then extracted everything you could from them. Food, minerals, ores, skilled workers—anything you could use, you took. You impressed people from my family's lands as young as sixteen into your 'army,' then used them as cannon fodder!"

"You traitor!"

"Traitor? I'm not the one holding people hostage to ensure they follow your ambitions! Soldiers of the Council, those of you who are not *Fylakes*! You have been used as cannon fodder to weaken your baron's power base while his stay strong! You don't think I'm telling the truth? Who led the assaults on Grizano and Zarko? Whose forces took heavy causalities while capturing Livada two months ago?"

"Shut up, you bastard!"

"Your Grace," Jennings said on the channel he shared with Vedet, "we are monitoring the communications between the different noble forces, and they're trying to corroborate Toliver's claims among themselves."

"Keep on them," Vedet murmured. "If we don't have to fight them, that's better for us."

"Look at these 'Mechs!" Toliver continued, swinging an arm toward the mercenaries. "Where were they when you assaulted Livada, Zarko, and Grizano? How many lives of your fellow soldiers could have been saved if one company, no, one *lance*, had been part of those assaults? But he didn't use them. Do you know why? Because he's been using them to terrify your barons into following him! He's been spending your lives to strengthen himself while weakening the rest of the Council!"

"Be quiet, impersonator!"

"Then come shut me up, coward!" the *Thunder Hawk* pointed at the *Titan II.* "I challenge you to a duel, Yiorgos! Graf on Graf! That's more of a chance than you gave my uncle. Face me one-on-one! Duke Brewer can witness our battle!"

"You're no graf! Just an impostor!"

"Patriarch Anton has recognized my right as Graf, as does Graf Oles Papandreouses, Baroness Mylonasa, and three other nobles."

"Interesting," Jennings said. "If he's telling the truth, he has the recognition of both the head of the Melissia Orthodox Church, a senior planetary noble, and several other nobles. That makes his claim very strong."

"You hide among the Republic scum!" Laskaris shouted.

Toliver's tone now carried anger. "Only because I didn't want to end up like my uncle! Shot at point-blank range while he was helpless!"

"You have no proof!"

"Your people made a mistake, Yiorgos. They wiped the *Thunder Hawk*'s main video storage drive, but not the secondary one. I have proof you executed my uncle—proof I'm releasing right now."

"Thomas," Vedet said. "Have the Guards ready to move."

"You *liar!*" Laskaris screamed. "A million kroner to the soldier who kills this *traitor!* Council forces, attack!"

A dozen mercenary 'Mechs charged forward, followed by several dozen *Fylakes* vehicles Other vehicles and 'Mechs were moving, but at right angles to the charge.

"Jennings!" Vedet barked. "What am I seeing here?"

"It appears the other noble forces are sitting this one out," The spymaster replied. "The young graf was most convincing."

"Thomas," Vedet said. "Change of plans. Pull back the Guards south and take up defensive positions."

"Your Grace!"

Something plummeted from the sky to Vedet's right, and he looked in that direction as an artillery shell landed between two of the charging mercenaries. A large explosion threw dirt into the air, sending one of the 'Mechs, a *Centurion,* reeling while the other one, a *Stinger,* skidded into the dirt with most of its right leg gone. A second round dropped on top of a *Fylakes* Minion hovertank. The vehicle exploded outward, the debris tearing into several surrounding vehicles.

In the few seconds Vedet had watched the artillery, the Guards had shifted south, the opposite direction the noble forces had moved. Vedet turned and moved toward the core of his forces, his bodyguards clustered around.

"Brewer!" Laskaris snarled. "Where are you going?"

"I've had my doubts about you, Yiorgos," Vedet said slowly. "I was willing to overlook the rumors, willing to overlook a few questionable things I've come across. But Graf Toliver's accusations are making me question this alliance."

"That man is a pretender!"

"He's piloting Graf Victor's *Thunder Hawk,* the one he died in."

"It was stolen!"

"My intelligence people have found nothing about that."

"You *believe him*?"

"He has raised questions," Vedet replied coolly, "enough questions for my people start an investigation."

"But that will take days!" Laskaris snarled.

"And you didn't accept his offer of a trial by combat."

"It was a trap!" Several more artillery rounds landed among the units charging Toliver, accenting Laskaris' claim.

"Maybe. Or maybe he expected you to do what you did— send your minions to kill him and prove his point about you."

Laskaris growled. "You're a fool! That *porni* got to you, didn't she? Always trying to get me into trouble!"

"Callisto?"

Laskaris laughed. "Intelligence reports placed her in Fillyra when you were recovering from your injuries. That's how she's operates—she worms her way into men's beds and bends them to her will."

It was Vedet's turn to laugh, a rich, deep one that make his ribs ache. "You are a fool," he said. "In my introduction letter, I said this wasn't my first time here on Melissia, and I that knew your mother."

"No…" Laskaris whispered. "It can't be. Callisto—"

"Is my *daughter.*" Vedet's words were as cold as a blizzard.

"No, no, *NO!* She's lying to you! She—"

"DNA confirms it. She is my flesh and blood, no doubt about it."

"I see." Laskaris's tone was hot with fury. "I'll have to put a couple of options into play sooner than later. See you in hell, Brewer."

For several seconds, there was silence, then—

"Your Grace!" Jason Boyens shouted. "My sensors are showing an attempted targeting lock-on on your *Atlas!*"

"Confirmed!" Goode shouted, the drawl gone.

"Direction?" Vedet barked

"Behind us! Bearing one seventy-six."

"Tufana!" Boyens shouted. "Range, three-fifty meters, moving southwest!"

Vedet glanced at the viewstrip and saw the fast-moving hovercraft flying across the rear of his Guards. Several of the rear guard, a battalion of heavy armor, were spinning their turrets around to confront the intruder.

"That Tufana must be spotting for artillery!" Neece shouted.

"We should move," Bronislaw growled.

"Echo Company!" Neece baked. "Switch on ECM!"

"Belay that! Leave them off until we get some idea what's being lobbed at us!" Vedet glanced in Laskaris' direction and saw the graf and his guards slow. *Anticipation,* he thought.

"Incoming contact!" Neece yelled. "Missiles!"

The duke's eyes flicked toward the aerial radar and saw several high-flying objects appearing on his screen. "ID?"

"Arrow IVs! Multiple Arrow IVs! ETA to impact, twenty seconds!"

"We should *definitely* move," Bronislaw growled even deeper.

Vedet scowled. "Echoes, spool up the ECM and move! Thomas, order an all-out attack on the *Fylakes!*" He put the *Atlas III* into a run, the rest of his bodyguard followed. Around him, the rest of the Hesperus Guards charged Laskaris' forces.

By now, the forces who had charged Toliver were falling back, battered by the intense artillery strikes. Toliver, in his *Thunder Hawk,* was leading a half dozen Republic 'Mechs and a company of armor in a charge across the crater-marred ground.

Vedet glanced at the radar and the oncoming missiles. "Midori, where did the Council get Arrow IV from? I don't recall them having any!"

Jennings' tone was calm and brisk. "The latest reports indicate when the Council overran Grizano and Zarko, they captured three Schiltron omni-tanks equipped with Arrow IVs. We had no reports they had trained people to use them."

Vedet scowled. "Thomas! You heard?"

"Yes, sir!" Kirk was more distracted and less calm than Jennings. "I've already sent a squadron of aerospace fighters to hunt them down!"

"Good! See if you can free up some hovertanks to chase down that Tufana and any other artillery spotters!"

The battle was becoming more chaotic, 'Mechs and vehicles firing and being hit by autocannons, missiles, lasers, and PPCs. The Guards' edge in training told as more *Fylakes* vehicles exploded or stopped moving and mercenaries' 'Mechs staggered from multiple hits.

"Arrow IV splashdown in three, two, one!"

The ground exploded around Vedet's bodyguards, digging deep holes into the ground and sending shrapnel, rocks, and dirt in every direction at bone-crushing and armor-denting velocity. Vedet felt some impacts, but the *Atlas III* was shielded from the worst of it.

"Your Grace!" Neece shouted. "Are you all right?"

Vedet glanced at his damage board. There were some small areas of yellow, but it was scattered across the entire *Atlas*. "I'm fine."

"Echo company!" Neece barked. "Status?"

"Still breathing," Goode said. "But old *Six-gun Annie* ain't doing so hot. Armor damage all along the left side."

"Ditto here," said Boyens. "Ax still works though."

"Keep your people close, Neece," Vedet muttered, glancing over to see Bronislaw still sitting on his shoulder. "Bronislaw, are you all right?"

"I am fine," the Elemental growled. "But the fight is not over."

"No, but I plan to change that, starting now."

CHAPTER 26

LOVELESS FOOTHILLS
JAHRESZEITWUNDER
MELISSIA
JADE FALCON OCCUPATION ZONE
8 MARCH, 3151

The space between the two forces had shrunk to where if a shot missed its intended target, it would likely hit another target in the tightly packed forces. Under Kirk's orders, the Guards had spread their lines to outflank the *Fylakes* and mercenaries.

"Bravo Two-Six to all Bravo Twos!" Walt shouted as he swung the turret of his Manticore II around to target a merc *Longbow.* "Concentrate fire by lances on the biggest target you can see! Lance commanders have the call. Bravo-One, we're taking on the *Longbow* at mark sixty-two!"

When the turret stopped, Walt was already peering through a viewfinder. "Parson! *Longbow* at bearing sixty-seven, range three hundred twenty meters!"

"Spotted!" Parsons called out. "On target!"

"Up!"

"Ready!"

"Fire!"

The Manticore's heavy PPC sent a brilliant bolt of blue lightning ripping into the assault 'Mech's left side. A heartbeat later, another heavy PPC blast and four streams of autocannon rounds smashed into the *Longbow*, sending the 85-ton 'Mech reeling, clipping a *Fylakes* Maxim and crashing into a mercenary *Chimera*, sending both 'Mechs to the ground.

Just then, something heavy slammed into the Manticore II's turret, the sound making Walt's head ring and his vision blur. "What the hell was that?"

"Patton, front left!" someone yelled.

Walt turned the turret around until the tank in question came into his sight. "Parson! Haynes!" he shouted, calling in the enhanced long-range missiles' operator and Parsons. "Patton at bearing three-four-seven, range two hundred meters!"

"Spotted!" Parsons called out. "On target!"

"Targeted!" Haynes called out.

"Up!"

"*Ready!*" both gunners called out

"Fire!"

The enhanced long-range missiles were designed to have half the minimum range of the normal LRMs. The result was they were effective at shorter ranges, and the twenty missiles that screamed from the Manticore II's launchers slammed into the Patton's turret and top with all the fury of an angry god. The Defiance 980 heavy PPC beam slammed into the left track, destroying a large section of track and shattering several of the track wheels.

The Patton came to a stop, just as more missiles and four streams of autocannon shells ripped into it. There was an explosion, and the Patton's turret lifted off its ring before crashing back down onto its body.

"Let's find the next target!" Walt growled, and he began doing just that.

Lisa Lee's lance was acting as a flank guard, so they were away from the main body when things went to hell. She had immediately moved to rejoin her company, but Hauptmann Hugo Klotz, her company commander, had directed her to protect the flank.

When the order to attack had come, she had started a series of hit-and-run attacks on the Flakes' new flank. There were only a few mercenary 'Mechs here, so the first attacks had been clean in-and-out attacks that had left destroyed and damaged vehicles. But someone on the other side had decided Lee and her lance were a danger.

"I've got a *Stinger* and a *Phoenix Hawk* on the right!" Harrigan shouted, his rotary autocannon spitting a short burst in that direction.

"Two *Spider*s on the left!" one of the Commisos shouted.

"Fall back!" Lisa shouted, targeting a merc *Nyx* and cutting loose with her light PPCs and the LRMs from her multi-missile launchers. One human-made lightning bolt slapped into the ground near the 30-ton enemy 'Mech, while the other one tore armor off the light 'Mech's left arm. The missiles shattered armor in several places, but it wasn't enough to slow it down. Lisa spotted a sixth 'Mech, a *Gravedigger*, lurking behind the *Nyx*.

She and her lance continued giving ground. "Gamma Three-Six to Gamma Six," she said. "I'm being pressed by the enemy, and we're outnumbered. Can you assist?"

"Negative, Three-Six, we have our hands full." Klotz sounded unhappy. "Wait five."

Lisa checked on the *Nyx*'s position, then targeted the *Gravedigger* and opened fire on it. A few missiles hit, and both PPC blasts missed. The *Gravedigger* returned fire, its PPC ripping away armor on the *Gauntlet*'s left torso and submunitions from the LB-X AC round from the denting armor to the left of Lisa's cockpit.

"Gamma Three-Six," Klotz said. "I have Angel Three-Three available Channel three-two-four."

"Thanks, Six." She changed channels. "Angel Three-Three, this is Gamma Three-Six. I need help."

"Give us your location, and we'll be there in a jiff." the voice replied. It was a low, smooth, and husky male voice.

An explosion nearby snapped out of her funk and glanced at her map screen. "Angel Three-One, map coordinates are—" She read off a long list of numbers.

"Copy, Gamma Three one. ETA is twenty seconds."

Lisa focused on the fight in front of her. Harrigan's *Storm Raider* was battered, but so were the *Stinger* and *Phoenix*

Hawk. From the amount of flames on her left, the twins were apparently trying to cook the *Spiders.*

"Gamma Three-Six, I'm seeing a lot of fire from your location. Can you confirm?"

"Confirm fire," Lisa replied. "That's my left flank."

"Copy, Three-Six. We'll be coming in from the southeast, moving northwest. Beginning strafing run now."

"Harrigan! Commisos!" Lisa shouted, forgoing radio call signs. "Break contact and head southwest, now! Friendly fighters coming in from the southeast!"

She spun her *Gauntlet-A* around and took off at a MASC-enhanced run. To her left, Harrigan let off a long burst with his RAC, then turned and dashed away. Plumes of plasmas showed the twins' efforts to break free. Lasers and missiles chased them, but they were opening the distance, and moving too fast for anything more than a few missile hits.

So intent on her escape, Lisa almost missed the pair of *Xerxes* that came screaming in, strafing the mercs. Heavy autocannons rounds and lasers ripped into the ground and mercenaries alike, sending smoke and flame into the air. Then, both fighters were screaming into the sky, pursued by a few missiles and lasers.

"That should do the job, Three-Six," the rich, warm voice replied.

Lisa turned and scanned the area. Three of the mercenaries were down. "Looks like it, Three-Three," she replied. "Thanks for the assist."

"You're welcome. I have another call to answer. Angel Three-Three out."

"Have two enemy lances off to the right!" one of the Commisos shouted.

Lisa looked in that direction and saw a half dozen light 'Mechs moving parallel to the battle. "Gamma Three-Six to Gamma Six. I've got a half dozen lights trying to outflank us."

"Can't help you, Three-six," Klotz replied. "Handle them on your own."

"Copy, Six. We'll keep them away." Lisa looked back at her lance. "We're it, people. One Commisos with me, the other with Harrigan. We're going to heat 'em up and burn 'em down.

Let's hit these guys hard enough to make 'em regret their life choices."

The battle was still raging. Even with the advantage in experience and unit cohesion, Vedet's Guards were still hard-pressed. The combat was a whirlwind of weapons fire, movement and dust kicked up by over a hundred 'Mechs and three times as many vehicles. At the core of the Guards, Vedet sat, surrounded by the four standing members of Echo Company.

"They're still coming!" Kirk shouted, triggering both his *Fafnir*'s heavy Gauss rifles at a Council *Phoenix Hawk*.

One Gauss round sped past the medium 'Mech's shoulder, and slammed into another Council 'Mech, a *Stinger*, ripping away most of the left side of the torso. The second round slammed into the *Phoenix Hawk*'s central torso, just below the cockpit, with enough force to crumple the central torso. It staggered back, right into the line of fire of Goreson's *Sunder-A*. The combination of the *Sunder*'s extended-range PPC, Gauss rifle, and several small swarms of long-range missiles pummeled the 45-ton 'Mech from shoulders to knees, dropping it onto its back. It didn't rise again.

Vedet looked at the map. The noble force had fallen back to a low rise to the north of the battle and sat there, watching. Two companies of 'Mechs, several regiments of armor and some battle armor. Not much, but maybe it was enough to change the balance.

"Toliver!" he shouted into the radio.

"What?" the young graf replied, his *Thunder Hawk* firing all three Gauss rifles at a merc *Rifleman*. Both rounds slammed into the 60-ton 'Mech, sending it to the ground with its left leg missing.

"The nobles that aren't fighting! Convince them to join us!"

"Me? You're a duke!"

"But I'm an outsider! You and Laskaris are the highest nobles left on the planet! If anyone's going to convince those nobles on that hill, it's going to be you or him!"

The *Thunder Hawk* took several steps back, firing its lasers at an advancing *Fylakes* Pegasus that looked battered, with sparks coming out from under its lift skirt.

The hovercraft fired a double-batch of SRMs at the Republic 'Mech, most of the dozen rounds finding armor across its torsos and legs. The *Thunder Hawk* cut loose with its lasers, three missing the still-moving vehicle, but the fourth one slashed open the lift skirt and found one of the fans inside. The Pegasus slewed to the right and slammed into a stopped *Fylakes* Vedette tank with enough force to crumple its nose and stall its engine.

Movement and explosions from his left caught Vedet's attention. "Incoming 'Mechs!" Neece yelled. "It's Laskaris and his people!"

Vedet turned, but a hard double impact sent the *Atlas III* staggering, forcing him to forget about anything else except staying on his feet. He gritted his teeth as his ribs protested as they strained against his harness. He planted his feet and the assault 'Mech quickly stabilized.

His head snapped around and he saw a knot of Council 'Mechs charging toward him and Echo Company. Laskaris' *Titan II* was in the center of the group, and a half dozen Grey Death heavy battle suits ran forward at their feet.

"Echo Company!" Neece shouted. "Form a wall! Protect the duke!" She planted her *BattleMaster* in front of the *Atlas II*, with Jason Boyens's *Berserker* forming up on her left, and Goode *Marauder* and Swanson's *Crusader* forming up on her right, all of them opening fire on the graf and his bodyguards. Vedet saw a flare of jump jets from his shoulder as Bronislaw leaped into the air, firing his suit's SRMs at the charging Council battle armor.

Vedet targeted the *Titan II* and opened fire with his rotary autocannon and Streak LRMs. The autocannon burst missed the Graf's 'Mech, instead ripping into a Council *Thug* that was shielding the noble, smashing armor across its right arm and torso. The streak LRMs also struck a shielding Council 'Mech, this one a *Zeus* that tore away armor around the 80-ton 'Mech's head.

Two of the graf's bodyguard 'Mechs, a *Thug* and an *Ostroc*, fell, while Goode's *Marauder* fell over, missing its right leg and most of its torso. Boyens' *Berserker* charged at the Council *Zeus*, ax raised high. Vedet opened fire with the *Atlas III*'s medium pulse lasers and SRMs at the *Zeus*. Two of his beams found armor while several of the short-range missiles exploded along the Council 'Mech's right shoulder to left hip. Bronislaw was among the Gray Death suits, firing his small laser and swinging his other arm like a man possessed.

The 80-ton 'Mech swayed like a drunk, just as the *Berserker* swung its huge weapon at it. The ax slammed into the *Zeus'* chest with enough force to split armor, leaving a two-meter-long, half-meter-wide gash behind. The *Zeus* fired its large laser into Jason Boyens' 'Mech, melting armor along the *Berserker*'s waist.

The *Ostroc* went down for good under the combined firepower of Neece and Swanson. That left Laskaris' *Titan II*, the *Zeus*, and a *Thunderbolt* standing for the Council, and the *Zeus* was under heavy assault by Boyens. Bronislaw, his suit scarred and battered, smashed his claw into the faceplate of a Gray Death battlesuit.

"Swanson, concentrate on the *Thunderbolt*!" Neece shouted. Echo Company's *BattleMaster* and *Crusader* open fire on the 65-ton Council 'Mech, covering it in missiles and cutting away armor with laser fire. Heat and smoke pouring out of it, the *Thunderbolt* fired back, and Swanson's *Crusader* exploded as ammunition cooked off. There was an ejection from the *Crusader*'s cockpit, but Vedet didn't notice which direction it went as the *Titan II* cut loose with its entire arsenal at Vedet. A heavy PPC beam, short-range missiles and laser blasted and melted away armor from the *Atlas'* legs and torso. Red lights flashed and warning buzzers went off as the assault 'Mech took internal damage, driving Vedet to one knee.

Vedet groaned, as his still-healing ribs flared in pain and his breathing became harder. He looked up in time to see Laskaris' *Titan II* stride toward him, determined to finish him. The *Zeus* was down, Jason Boyens's hatchet buried in its cockpit, while Neece was squaring off against the *Thunderbolt*, exchanging fire and physical blows with abandon.

"It's over, Brewer!" Laskaris bellowed, bring his arm-mounted heavy PPC up for a point-blank shot. "You die here, a traitor and—"

The *Titan II* staggered as two Gauss rifle rounds slammed into its left arm and torso, amputating the left arm at the shoulder and ripping open the left side of the torso.

"That's for my uncle, you murderer!" Toliver snarled.

"You bastard!" Laskaris screamed.

Ignoring the pain, Vedet pushed himself to his feet, brought the *Atlas'* rotary autocannon up and jammed his finger on the trigger. The Mydron-RS whirled and spat out a long burst before it cut off in mid-burst as the weapon jammed. The swarm of slugs ripped into the *Titan's* upper chest and head, smashing the canopy into fragments. Then, Boyens swung his *Berserker's* ax and struck the *Titan* from behind, the seven-ton hatchet smashing through the 'Mech's back. Laskaris' 'Mech froze, then topped over and slammed into the ground.

Bronislaw, his battered suit barely functional, limped over to the downed 'Mech and looked inside the shattered cockpit. "The graf is dead," he said, sounding tired.

"You sure?" Bowens asked.

"Body parts do not count as alive."

"Attention everyone!" Vedet called out on the radio, "Graf Laskaris is dead! Cease fire! The graf is dead. This battle is over! Council forces, surrender!"

He closed his eyes, leaned back in his chair as Neece and Boyens walked over to stand next to him, fighting the wave of pain that threatened to shove him into obliviousness.

"Graf Laskaris is down!" Toliver shouted. "*Fylakes*, surrender, or we will destroy you! Surrender, and you will be treated fairly! You have one minute to comply!"

More and more of the Hesperus Guards took up the call, and the weapons fire died away. Silence fell across the battlefield.

Vedet opened his eyes. "Thomas?"

"Yes, Your Grace?"

"Take charge of the surrender. Get a medical team over here as soon as possible."

"Are you wounded?"

"Nothing new...but I probably shouldn't have gotten back into the cockpit until I finished healing."

"Understood, Your Grace. Med team is on the way."

Vedet nodded and closed his eyes again.

CHAPTER 27

EUROPA
JAHRESZEITWUNDER
MELISSIA
JADE FALCON OCCUPATION ZONE
30 MARCH 3151

"They are ready for you, Your Grace."

Brewer looked up from his speech and nodded to Kirk. "Thank you, Thomas."

He stood slowly, wincing as a flash of pain reminded him his ribs were still tender, despite the brace he was wearing under his high-collared tunic. His shoulder also ached, but it was getting better. Dr. Ginley's opinion of Vedet getting into a cockpit so soon after nearly being killed had been a profanity-laced tirade that had made even Bronislaw wary of the man for a week afterward.

So, he had been confined to bed for the next two weeks, while Foster and Leeson led the negotiations, with Vedet watching via vidscreen. Once he had been allowed to move around, Vedet had taken a more active part in the discussions, as both the Republic and the Council reluctantly hammered out an agreement to end the war and come together.

Outside the room, Bronislaw, wearing a suit, but still carrying the support machine gun, waited with him, along with the mobile members of Echo Company. Both Wills and Goode were still in the hospital, recovering from their wounds. Somehow, all six had survived, but none of their 'Mechs would be ready for combat soon.

Surrounded by the four Guards soldiers and trailed by Bronislaw, they started down the hall to the Parliament chamber. The route was lined with Hesperus Guards infantry every five meters, presenting arms as the group passed them. Vedet purposefully ignored the camera drones that hovered above and in front of them. This speech was going to be broadcast planet-wide, so this was part of the show.

At the next intersection, eight officers in dress uniforms stood at attention. Kirk had chosen these officers for their performance under fire to command units inside the expanding Hesperus Guards. Vedet recognized Kommandant McWalsh and Hauptmann Lee, as Kirk had put both of them at the top of the promotion list. The eight waited until Vedet's group had passed, then fell in behind them in two rows of four.

As they reached the chamber doors, the five-meter-tall doors were pulled open by two uniformed doormen. As they crossed the threshold, Vedet could see the room was packed— nobles on one side, Republic supporters on the other, and the galleys filled with ordinary civilians.

The sergeant-at-arms, a short, barrel-chested man with snow-white hair, rapped his staff. "My lords, ladies, and civilians. The Duke of Hesperus II, Vedet Gerald Greydon Brewer!"

Vedet left his bodyguards back at the entrance and walked forward, scanning the crowd as he did so. He saw a mix of emotions; anger, hope, indifference, and neutral interest. He saw both Kerr and Dyhr on the noble side of the chamber; Pocasio had vanished, and despite Jennings' best efforts, couldn't be found.

The chamber was silent as he walked to the speaker's podium, which stood alone below the Speaker of the Parliament desk. He glanced toward the Republic side and saw Callisto standing next to Mendez, wearing a simple yet elegant dark blue dress, and looking so much like her mother, it made his heart ache. Toliver was standing at the base of the speaker's podium, wearing the blue and sea-green of House Toliver, looking more noble than any other time Vedet had seen him. As they got close, they nodded to each other.

Vedet climbed the stairs slowly. Once he was at the stand, he placed the leather folder with his speech on the shelf and opened it. He scanned the first page of notes, then looked up at the waiting crowd. "Citizens of Melissia. The war between the Noble Council and the Melissia Republic is over."

He looked around the room. "But this is just the first step. We have many wounds that need healing, and there are hurt feelings on both sides. I understand that, but it is time we step beyond all of that. We don't have time for a period of gentle healing, not with the threats that lurk out there. We don't know for sure if or when the Jade Falcons will return, or whether the roving eye of the Hell's Horses or the Ghost Bears will look in our direction."

"What about the Commonwealth?" someone shouted from the noble side of the chamber.

Vedet turned toward where the question had come from. "What about it?" he asked, keeping his tone strong, but even. "The Commonwealth is weak, and fighting to hold on to what they already have. They have neither the time nor the resources to reclaim those worlds they have lost in the last ten years. The cold reality is the Commonwealth is not coming to save us. If Melissia is to be saved, it must be the people here that do that."

"An off-world noble!" this shout was from the Republic side of the chamber. "And a failed Archon at that!"

Vedet shifted to look at the Republicans. "You and the Council were doing *so* well before I arrived," he said, his voice heavy with sarcasm. "Too busy fighting over petty matters."

"The nobles are parasites!"

"And the Republic is nothing but power-hungry bastards!"

The chamber exploded in angry voices, shouts, and screams. The speaker, a heavy-set man with a florid face, banged a wooden hammer, but the sound was lost in the bedlam of anger.

Bronislaw stepped forward, his machine gun pointing into the air, and bellowed, *"QUIET!"* The thunderous shout cut through all other sounds with the sharpness of a knife and the sound stopped.

The Elemental scanned the room, his glare making him look even more menacing. "The Duke will speak, and you will listen!"

Vedet nodded to his bodyguard, who stepped back, the machine gun barrel still pointing in the air. He let the silence linger for a few seconds before he continued. "You just made my point, ladies and gentlemen. The time for hate and distrust is past. If Melissia is to survive as a free world, *we* must put everything aside and work together. To facilitate that, this is the new government that will govern Melissia, one that is neither Commonwealth nor Clan. The Republic will remain, but henceforth will include the former Council lands as districts in the new Parliament, and return to its name as the House of Commons. In addition, we will reestablish the House of Nobles as Parliament's upper house. We will hold elections in two months to bring these districts into the Parliament."

There was a round of angry muttering from the Republic side. With the new members, the Freedom Party would lose power and put their agenda in danger. Jennings was already digging into the party organization, zeroing in on anyone who might turn to violence to hold onto what they had.

Vedet let the muttering go for a few seconds, then said, "In addition, all noble lands are to remain with the families who hold them, and any lands seized by the Republic or Council from those families are to be returned to them in the same condition they were before their seizure."

That brought on another round of muttering from the Republic and a few on the Council side. That was something that would take years of court cases to sort out. No matter. Vedet continued. "But this is more than Melissia. There are seven other worlds only a jump away, another thirteen two jumps away."

He took a deep breath. "Melissia was a district capital, and it can be a new capital, of an independent state, made up of planets that the Commonwealth has given up on." He looked around the chamber. "But there is no telling what shape these words around us are in. Some may be like Melissia, at war with themselves. Others may still be under nominal Falcon control, while others could be under control of warlords. We must reach out to these worlds to show them they are not alone in the darkness.

"Therefore, today I am declaring the formation of a new state—the Vesper Marches."

He let the words sink in. There was a mix of puzzlement and confusion among the audience, but he had their attention. "In that spirit, those members of the Council and Republic forces militaries who are not accused of war crimes and wish to serve will be integrated into the Melissia Defense Force, under the leadership of Graf Matthew Toliver, become part of the Hesperus Guards, or become part of the new Vesper Marches Armed Forces."

Vedet looked at the Noble side of the house. "While your lands are secured here on Melissia, I will have need of your service beyond this system. Many of those worlds we seek to gather under our aegis may no longer have a viable noble class to rely on. As on Melissia, it is probable that some families were wiped out, while others fled or have been reduced to serfdom by an uncaring Clan. While the surviving families will be given their chance to reclaim their titles, there will be openings for those of you willing to journey to new worlds." He smiled. "After all, while remain barons if you can become landgraves and grafs?"

A buzz of excitement came from the assembled nobles, and Vedet smiled before looking around the chamber again. "We are still working out the details, and we ask for your patience as we construct our new state. However, we welcome your input and seek your council."

He inhaled again. "I, Duke Vedet Brewer, declare the Vesper Marches as a safeguard for its people against the fall of night. It is time for a new course and the seas will be rough. But together we can come through this, stronger, more united and ready to face whatever the universe dares throw at us. Thank you, and God bless us all."

He closed the folder and stepped down from the speaker's podium. There was applause, not a rousing, cheering sort of reaction, but better than he had feared.

Vedet nodded to Toliver as he walked past him and, surrounded by Echo Company and Bronislaw, left the chamber. He didn't stop to speak to anyone—there was still too much raw emotion in the crowd. He would talk to who he needed to that night.

The reception at the margrave's palace that evening was supposed to be a time to relax and celebrate. But for Vedet, the event was a working one. He had enough support from both the Republic and the Council to feel secure in his new position as the leader of the Vesper Marches, but the more support he had, the better.

Besides, his work was just now truly beginning. Jennings and Kirk were already organizing teams to investigate and secure nearby planets—there was a force already on the way to Chapultepec to bring them into the new state. The new military was starting with the combined forces of the Republic and Council forces, overseen by First Hesperus drill sergeants, going back into training and molded into reliable troops. The best—those who passed Jennings' background checks—would become part of the Hesperus Guards. The rest would be split between the Melissian Defense Force and the Vesper Marches Armed Forces.

Under doctor's orders, Vedet sat in a chair in an alcove, Bronislaw standing behind the chair, without the machine gun. A chair sat across from him, close enough for quiet conversations. Outside the alcove, the four members of Echo Company stood, engaging in conversations with anyone who wondered by.

The conversations had proven fruitful so far. Several members from both sides had sat with Vedet and discussed their concerns and problems. He, in turn, had listened and discussed the matters in an easy, but confident manner. More often than not, the person Vedet talked to went away with more hope than they had when they had first sat down.

Vedet was sipping a glass of wine when Matthew Toliver came over and sat down in the empty chair. "Your Grace."

"Graf," Vedet replied seriously. "How can I help you?"

Toliver glanced around, looked at Bronislaw and exhaled slowly. "I think it's time for that talk, sir."

Vedet cocked an eyebrow and looked out over the crown until he spotted Callisto standing across the room, taking to a couple of women. She wore a flowing dress in the green and gold of House Mylonasa. He looked back at Toliver, who was also watching Callisto. "What are your intentions toward my daughter, Graf?"

Toliver looked back at him. "I want to marry her, sir. With your permission."

"You're asking the wrong person. I know from experience that Mylonasa women are independent and difficult to persuade."

"I shall do my best, sir."

"Do you have an engagement ring yet?"

Toliver shook his head. "I haven't had the time to find one. If I had one, I would do it tonight."

"Really?" Vedet reached under his shirt and pulled out the necklace. He slid the ring off the chair and handed the ring to Toliver. "Thirty years ago, I asked Callisto's mother to marry me. Circumstances beyond both of our control prevented that from happening. I've held onto this ring for thirty years, in a hope that will never happen now. It's time I passed it onto someone who needs it more than I do."

"No, sir, I can't—"

Vedet shook his head. "Its time with me has ended. It's time for a new start, with a new love. Take it, Matthew...take it, and make my daughter happy."

Slowly, Toliver reached out and took the ring. He stood slowly and bowed. "I will, sir." He turned on his heel and marched toward the woman he loved. Conversation died as he passed, and all eyes went to him as he approached Callisto.

She didn't realize what was happening until she looked up and saw Toliver bearing down on her. The women she was talking with looked back at him and immediately moved out of the way, leaving the couple staring at each other.

The room fell silent, the stillness lingering for a few seconds before Toliver came to full attention. "Baroness Mylonasa," he said. "You have been so much of my life these past few months, and before that, as we grew up together. I—"

He swallowed and sank to one knee, presenting the ring to her. "Callisto Mylonasa, my heart is already yours. Will you marry me?"

Callisto stared at the ring for several seconds, then looked up at Vedet, asking about the ring with her eyes. Vedet nodded, and she looked down at Toliver. "Y-Yes," she said. "Yes, I will!"

Toliver rose to his feet just in time to catch Callisto as she flung himself into his arms, kissing him fiercely. The rest of the guests began clapping in appreciation.

Vedet felt his eyes tear up as he watched them. *I wish you were here, Cassie,* he thought, a tear rolling down his cheek. He closed his eyes. *Our girl is grown up.*

He felt a feminine hand gently caress his shoulder, but when he reached for it, he found nothing. He opened his eyes and stood. "I'm going out for some air."

"Yes, sir," Bronislaw replied and followed Vedet out of the room.

The palace was on the edge of the city. It was heavily guarded, so Vedet felt safe when he walked out onto the balcony. Bronislaw stayed near the door, a silent, immoveable statue.

There, on the balcony, Vedet Brewer, duke, former Archon, and known as a villain throughout most of the Commonwealth, finally let himself cry. Cry for a lost love, for a daughter he never saw grow up, and for a life he was fated never to live.

Two months of iron control broke as he finally let the bottled-up emotions loose. Once started, the tears didn't stop coming as everything he'd missed out on crashed down on him. He cursed the Laskaris family, his own father, and anyone he could think of that had kept him and Cassie apart.

He was so wrapped up in his grief and anger, he didn't feel the hand on his shoulder at first. When he felt it and he reached up and touched it, he felt a warm hand. He turned and found Callisto standing there, concern on her face. "Father?"

Without thinking, he reached out and pulled her into a tight hug. "I miss her," he choked out.

She returned his hug. "Me, too."

"I should have come back for her—and you. I should have told the Laskaris family to go to hell and taken both of you home to Hesperus II."

"Her parents would have charged you with kidnapping."

"That wouldn't have stopped me."

"You can't change the past. We can only live to change the future."

They held each other for a long time, united by a woman who was longer alive, yet who had left a deep mark on both of them.

Finally, Vedet released his daughter and looked at her. "This is where I met her for the first time," he said, placing his hand on the stone railing. He used his other hand to wipe away his tears with his other hand. "Here, on this balcony. She was wearing a teal silk dress that glowed in the moonlight. Her hair was done in a long French braid, with diamond strings woven through it. She had an aura about her that made me immediately intrigued with her."

"Not love at first sight?" Castillo asked in a teasing tone.

He smiled. "I saw several men approach her during the evening, only to be turned down with a dismissive glare. I thought to myself, 'There is a woman who knows what she wants and won't settle for anything less.'" He chuckled. "Later that evening, she came right up to me and introduced herself."

Callisto smiled. "That was Mother."

"I spent two months here, most of it with her. After two weeks, I was in love with her. Another week, and she told me she was in love with me. We kept our romance quiet, so only a few people knew about us. Our dates were in out-of-the-way places, and we were just a couple in love."

"Then Priam took her away from you."

Vedet nodded, and said in a soft, bitter tone, "We made love that last night, and when she left me that morning, it was the last time I saw her." He took a deep breath. "There's always been a hole in my heart since that day, and she has never been far from my thoughts. Several times, I could almost hear her voice scolding me for some stupid decision I'd made."

He shook his head. "Without her, I was half the man I should have been. She would have told me the truth as she saw it, and no doubt saved me from many bad decisions I've made over the years. Being here, being with you...reminds me just how much I miss her."

Callisto hugged his arm. "Me, too."

"I want to visit her grave," he said. "I need to talk to her, to tell her everything I've done."

She nodded. "I can arrange that. When?"

"Next week."

"Okay."

"Come with me?"

"Of course."

"Bring Matthew."

She nodded. "I will."

Vedet stepped back and gripped her hands. "He's a good choice. Don't make the same mistakes we made."

She smiled. "I won't."

Vedet looked toward the doorway and saw Toliver standing there next to Bronislaw. "I think we should return to the reception."

"Not before you dry your eyes—Father."

He smiled. "Are you okay with not being publicly acknowledged as my daughter?"

"The time will come when I will stand by you as your daughter. But now isn't that time. We all have work to do."

He nodded. "Then let's do it together."

EPILOGUE

"You failed."

The mostly dark chamber was somewhere in the hills east of Tabatinga. Iago Pocasio didn't know where it was, and standing in the middle of the chamber, he didn't really care.

There were nine other people here with him. Four were guards, wearing white robes and holding electrostaffs. Two were behind Pocasio and two in front of him.

Sitting on a stone platform two meters above the chamber floor, the other five sat in shadow. Pocasio only knew them by their number. One, the committee leader, was in the middle, with Three and Five to Pocasio's right and Two and Four to his left.

Pocasio swung his head to stare at the male speaker, Five. "There was interference from Brewer."

"An excuse."

"The plan did not account for him or his Guards."

"He unraveled years of work in only a couple of months!"

"Enough," the center figure said. It was a woman's voice, carrying authority. "This is not the time to attach blame. Pocasio is right, Five; the plan did not account for outside interference."

"It should have," Five replied.

"One is right," the one of the far left, Four, said. He was also male, with a slight Germanic accent. "As is Five. We allowed our arrogance to cloud our judgment on this matter."

"But we need Melissia!" Five snapped. "We have to reverse this!"

"What would you suggest?" One asked. "We have no military, nor do we have the funds to hire mercenaries."

"We could hire an assassin," Five said.

"It will take time to find such a person," Two said. She was also a woman and sounded younger than the others. "More time to arrange the equipment and payment."

"We need to take action now!" Five snarled.

"We would need an expert assassin to accomplish this task, Five," Four said. "They are difficult to find and expensive to hire. Now, unless you know where there's a division of combat troops ready to go at a moment's notice, we must take another tack."

"We could choose another target," Three said. He had a raspy voice. "Melissia was our choice because of its former importance as a district capital."

"We could continue using Medellin as our base of operations."

"We cannot expand much more here before the LIC notices us," One said. "Melissia was perfect because the LIC presence is limited there."

"The forming of these small states in the former Falcon territory is making our job harder," Four said.

"We could expand our efforts into these new states," Pocasio said. "Most don't have a solid counter-intelligence service and if we move fast, we can set up cells on those planets and expand slowly. It wouldn't be as efficient as using Melissia as our main hub, but it would spread our influence wider, if not at the level we wanted."

"We should consider that," Four said.

"Agreed," Two said. "Better to change tactics and continue with the plan than to get fixated on a mistake we cannot correct now."

"But we still need to take out Brewer," Five said.

"Why don't you handle that, Iago?" One said.

"His last assassination attempt went so well," Five growled.

"I was forced to improvise," Pocasio said.

"We will leave the assassination in your hands," One said. "Find your assassin, then make the arrangements."

Pocasio frowned. "That will take some time. Besides the assassin, I need to groom the right figurehead to take over once Brewer is dead. I can't do that quickly."

"We will be patient. Take your time. We will move into these new worlds and establish cells, but Melissia is still the cornerstone of our plans. Eventually, we will need that planet."

Pocasio bowed. "I will start right away."

"You are dismissed. The Peace of Blake go with you."

"And may Blake guide our hands," Pocasio replied before he turned and walked out of the chamber.

ARCTIC FOX
LIGHT—30 TONS

ATLAS III
ASSAULT—100 TONS

BATTLEMASTER
ASSAULT—85 TONS

BERSERKER
ASSAULT—100 TONS

COMMANDO
Light—25 tons

CRUSADER
Heavy—65 tons

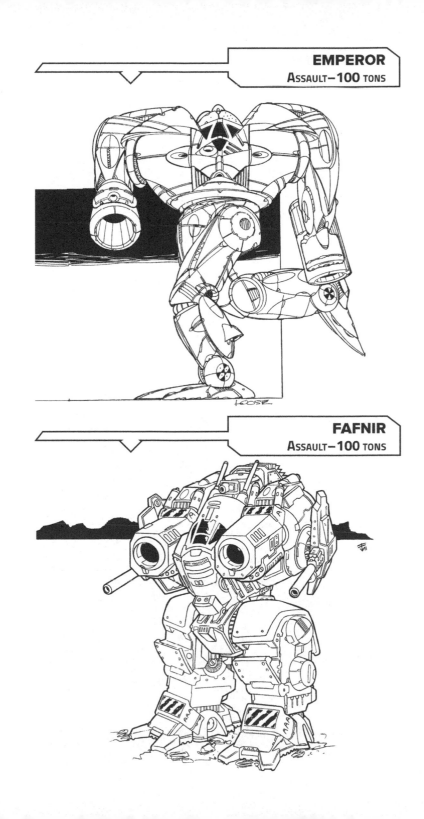

EMPEROR
ASSAULT–100 TONS

FAFNIR
ASSAULT–100 TONS

FIRESTARTER
LIGHT—35 TONS

GAUNTLET
MEDIUM—55 TONS

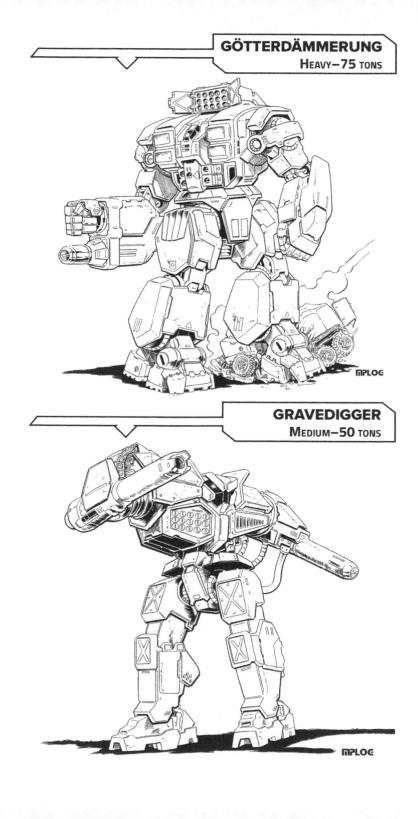

GÖTTERDÄMMERUNG
HEAVY—75 TONS

GRAVEDIGGER
MEDIUM—50 TONS

GRIFFIN
MEDIUM—55 TONS

ACS

LONGBOW
ASSAULT—85 TONS

MARAURDER
HEAVY—75 TONS

ACS

OSTROC
HEAVY—60 TONS

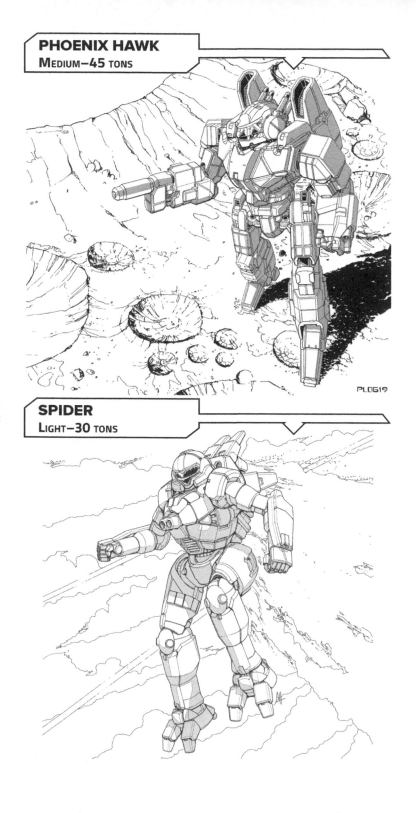

PHOENIX HAWK
MEDIUM—45 TONS

PLOG19

SPIDER
LIGHT—30 TONS

STINGER
LIGHT—20 TONS

STORM RAIDER
LIGHT—35 TONS

SUNDER
Assault—90 tons

THUNDER HAWK
Assault—100 tons

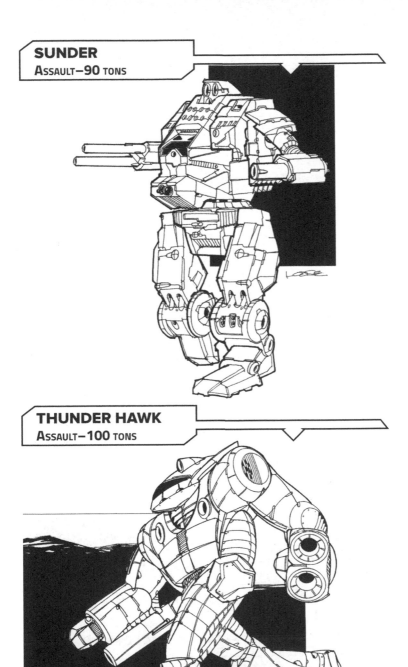

THUNDERBOLT
HEAVY—65 TONS

TITAN II
ASSAULT—100 TONS

ZEUS
ASSAULT—80 TONS

BATTLETECH GLOSSARY

AUTOCANNON

A rapid-fire, auto-loading weapon. Light autocannons range from 30 to 90 millimeter (mm), and heavy autocannons may be from 80 to 120mm or more. They fire high-speed streams of high-explosive, armor-piercing shells.

BATTLEMECH

BattleMechs are the most powerful war machines ever built. First developed by Terran scientists and engineers, these huge vehicles are faster, more mobile, better-armored and more heavily armed than any twentieth-century tank. Ten to twelve meters tall and equipped with particle projection cannons, lasers, rapid-fire autocannon and missiles, they pack enough firepower to flatten anything but another BattleMech. A small fusion reactor provides virtually unlimited power, and BattleMechs can be adapted to fight in environments ranging from sun-baked deserts to subzero arctic icefields.

DROPSHIPS

Because interstellar JumpShips must avoid entering the heart of a solar system, they must "dock" in space at a considerable distance from a system's inhabited worlds. DropShips were developed for interplanetary travel. As the name implies, a DropShip is attached to hardpoints on the JumpShip's drive core, later to be dropped from the parent vessel after in-system entry. Though incapable of FTL travel, DropShips are highly maneuverable, well-armed and sufficiently aerodynamic to take off from and land on a planetary surface. The journey from the jump point to the inhabited worlds of a system usually requires a normal-space journey of several days or weeks, depending on the type of star.

FLAMER

Flamethrowers are a small but time-honored anti-infantry weapon in vehicular arsenals. Whether fusion-based or fuel-based, flamers spew fire in a tight beam that "splashes" against a target, igniting almost anything it touches.

GAUSS RIFLE

This weapon uses magnetic coils to accelerate a solid nickel-ferrous slug about the size of a football at an enemy target, inflicting massive damage through sheer kinetic impact at long range and with little heat. However, the accelerator coils and the slug's supersonic speed mean that while the Gauss rifle is smokeless and lacks the flash of an autocannon, it has a much more potent report that can shatter glass.

INDUSTRIALMECH

Also known as WorkMechs or UtilityMechs, they are large, bipedal or quadrupedal machines used for industrial purposes (hence the name). They are similar in shape to BattleMechs, which they predate, and feature many of the same technologies, but are built for non-combat tasks such as construction, farming, and policing.

JUMPSHIPS

Interstellar travel is accomplished via JumpShips, first developed in the twenty-second century. These somewhat ungainly vessels consist of a long, thin drive core and a sail resembling an enormous parasol, which can extend up to a kilometer in width. The ship is named for its ability to "jump" instantaneously across vast distances of space. After making its jump, the ship cannot travel until it has recharged by gathering up more solar energy.

The JumpShip's enormous sail is constructed from a special metal that absorbs vast quantities of electromagnetic energy from the nearest star. When it has soaked up enough energy, the sail transfers it to the drive core, which converts it into a space-twisting field. An instant later, the ship arrives at the next jump point, a distance of up to thirty light-years. This field is known as hyperspace, and its discovery opened to mankind the gateway to the stars.

JumpShips never land on planets. Interplanetary travel is carried out by DropShips, vessels that are attached to the JumpShip until arrival at the jump point.

LASER

An acronym for "Light Amplification through Stimulated Emission of Radiation." When used as a weapon, the laser damages the target by concentrating extreme heat onto a small area. BattleMech lasers are designated as small, medium or large. Lasers are also available as shoulder-fired weapons operating from a portable backpack power unit. Certain range-finders and targeting equipment also employ low-level lasers.

LRM

Abbreviation for "Long-Range Missile," an indirect-fire missile with a high-explosive warhead.

MACHINE GUN

A small autocannon intended for anti-personnel assaults. Typically non-armor-penetrating, machine guns are often best used against infantry, as they can spray a large area with relatively inexpensive fire.

PARTICLE PROJECTION CANNON (PPC)

One of the most powerful and long-range energy weapons on the battlefield, a PPC fires a stream of charged particles that outwardly functions as a bright blue laser, but also throws off enough static discharge to resemble a bolt of manmade lightning. The kinetic and heat impact of a PPC is enough to cause the vaporization of armor and structure alike, and most PPCs have the power to kill a pilot in his machine through an armor-penetrating headshot.

SRM

The abbreviation for "Short-Range Missile," a direct-trajectory missile with high-explosive or armor-piercing explosive warheads. They have a range of less than one kilometer and are only reliably accurate at ranges of less than 300 meters. They are more powerful, however, than LRMs.

SUCCESSOR LORDS

After the fall of the first Star League, the remaining members of the High Council each asserted his or her right to become First Lord. Their star empires became known as the Successor States and the rulers as Successor Lords. The Clan Invasion temporarily interrupted centuries of warfare known as the Succession Wars, which first began in 2786.

BATTLETECH ERAS

The *BattleTech* universe is a living, vibrant entity that grows each year as more sourcebooks and fiction are published. A dynamic universe, its setting and characters evolve over time within a highly detailed continuity framework, bringing everything to life in a way a static game universe cannot match.

To help quickly and easily convey the timeline of the universe—and to allow a player to easily "plug in" a given novel or sourcebook—we've divided *BattleTech* into eight major eras.

STAR LEAGUE
(Present–2780)

Ian Cameron, ruler of the Terran Hegemony, concludes decades of tireless effort with the creation of the Star League, a political and military alliance between all Great Houses and the Hegemony. Star League armed forces immediately launch the Reunification War, forcing the Periphery realms to join. For the next two centuries, humanity experiences a golden age across the thousand light-years of human-occupied space known as the Inner Sphere. It also sees the creation of the most powerful military in human history.

(This era also covers the centuries before the founding of the Star League in 2571, most notably the Age of War.)

SUCCESSION WARS
(2781–3049)

Every last member of First Lord Richard Cameron's family is killed during a coup launched by Stefan Amaris. Following the thirteen-year war to unseat him, the rulers of each of the five Great Houses disband the Star League. General Aleksandr Kerensky departs with eighty percent of the Star League Defense Force beyond known space and the Inner Sphere collapses into centuries of warfare known as the Succession Wars that will eventually result in a massive loss of technology across most worlds.

CLAN INVASION
(3050–3061)

A mysterious invading force strikes the coreward region of the Inner Sphere. The invaders, called the Clans, are descendants of Kerensky's SLDF troops, forged into a society dedicated to becoming the greatest fighting force in history. With vastly superior technology and warriors, the Clans conquer world after world. Eventually this outside threat will forge a new Star League, something hundreds of years of warfare failed to accomplish. In addition, the Clans will act as a catalyst for a technological renaissance.

CIVIL WAR
(3062–3067)

The Clan threat is eventually lessened with the complete destruction of a Clan. With that massive external threat apparently neutralized, internal conflicts explode around the Inner Sphere. House Liao conquers its former Commonality, the St. Ives Compact; a rebellion of military units belonging to House Kurita sparks a war with their powerful border enemy, Clan Ghost Bear; the fabulously powerful Federated Commonwealth of House Steiner and House Davion collapses into five long years of bitter civil war.

JIHAD
(3067–3080)

Following the Federated Commonwealth Civil War, the leaders of the Great Houses meet and disband the new Star League, declaring it a sham. The pseudo-religious Word of Blake—a splinter group of ComStar, the protectors and controllers of interstellar communication—launch the Jihad: an interstellar war that pits every faction against each other and even against themselves, as weapons of mass destruction are used for the first time in centuries while new and frightening technologies are also unleashed.

DARK AGE
(3081–3150)

Under the guidance of Devlin Stone, the Republic of the Sphere is born at the heart of the Inner Sphere following the Jihad. One of the more extensive periods of peace begins to break out as the 32nd century dawns. The factions, to one degree or another, embrace disarmament, and the massive armies of the Succession Wars begin to fade. However, in 3132 eighty percent of interstellar communications collapses, throwing the universe into chaos. Wars erupt almost immediately, and the factions begin rebuilding their armies.

ILCLAN
(3151–present)

The once-invulnerable Republic of the Sphere lies in ruins, torn apart by the Great Houses and the Clans as they wage war against each other on a scale not seen in nearly a century. Mercenaries flourish once more, selling their might to the highest bidder. As Fortress Republic collapses, the Clans race toward Terra to claim their long-denied birthright and create a supreme authority that will fulfill the dream of Aleksandr Kerensky and rule the Inner Sphere by any means necessary: The ilClan.

CLAN HOMEWORLDS
(2786–present)

In 2784, General Aleksandr Kerensky launched Operation Exodus, and led most of the Star League Defense Force out of the Inner Sphere in a search for a new world, far away from the strife of the Great Houses. After more than two years and thousands of light years, they arrived at the Pentagon Worlds. Over the next two-and-a-half centuries, internal dissent and civil war led to the creation of a brutal new society—the Clans. And in 3049, they returned to the Inner Sphere with one goal—the complete conquest of the Great Houses.

LOOKING FOR MORE HARD HITTING BATTLETECH FICTION?

WE'LL GET YOU RIGHT BACK INTO THE BATTLE!

Catalyst Game Labs brings you the very best in *BattleTech* fiction, available at most ebook retailers, including Amazon, Apple Books, Kobo, Barnes & Noble, and more!

NOVELS

1. *Decision at Thunder Rift* by William H. Keith Jr.
2. *Mercenary's Star* by William H. Keith Jr.
3. *The Price of Glory* by William H. Keith, Jr.
4. *Warrior: En Garde* by Michael A. Stackpole
5. *Warrior: Riposte* by Michael A. Stackpole
6. *Warrior: Coupé* by Michael A. Stackpole
7. Wolves on the Border by Robert N. Charrette
8. *Heir to the Dragon* by Robert N. Charrette
9. *Lethal Heritage* (The Blood of Kerensky, Volume 1) by Michael A. Stackpole
10. *Blood Legacy* (The Blood of Kerensky, Volume 2) by Michael A. Stackpole
11. *Lost Destiny* (The Blood of Kerensky, Volume 3) by Michael A. Stackpole
12. *Way of the Clans* (Legend of the Jade Phoenix, Volume 1) by Robert Thurston
13. *Bloodname* (Legend of the Jade Phoenix, Volume 2) by Robert Thurston
14. *Falcon Guard* (Legend of the Jade Phoenix, Volume 3) by Robert Thurston
15. *Wolf Pack* by Robert N. Charrette
16. *Main Event* by James D. Long
17. *Natural Selection* by Michael A. Stackpole
18. *Assumption of Risk* by Michael A. Stackpole
19. *Blood of Heroes* by Andrew Keith
20. *Close Quarters* by Victor Milán
21. *Far Country* by Peter L. Rice
22. *D.R.T.* by James D. Long
23. *Tactics of Duty* by William H. Keith
24. *Bred for War* by Michael A. Stackpole
25. *I Am Jade Falcon* by Robert Thurston
26. *Highlander Gambit* by Blaine Lee Pardoe
27. *Hearts of Chaos* by Victor Milán
28. *Operation Excalibur* by William H. Keith
29. *Malicious Intent* by Michael A. Stackpole
30. *Black Dragon* by Victor Milán
31. *Impetus of War* by Blaine Lee Pardoe
32. *Double-Blind* by Loren L. Coleman
33. *Binding Force* by Loren L. Coleman
34. *Exodus Road* (Twilight of the Clans, Volume 1) by Blaine Lee Pardoe
35. *Grave Covenant* ((Twilight of the Clans, Volume 2) by Michael A. Stackpole

76. *Daughter of the Dragon* by Ilsa J. Bick
77. *Heretic's Faith* by Randall N. Bills
78. *Fortress Republic* by Loren L. Coleman
79. *Blood Avatar* by Ilsa J. Bick
80. *Trial by Chaos* by J. Steven York
81. *Principles of Desolation* by Jason M. Hardy and Randall N. Bills
82. *Wolf Hunters* by Kevin Killiany
83. *Surrender Your Dreams* by Blaine Lee Pardoe
84. *Dragon Rising* by Ilsa J. Bick
85. *Masters of War* by Michael A. Stackpole
86. *A Rending of Falcons* by Victor Milán
87. *Pandora's Gambit* by Randall N. Bills
88. *The Last Charge* by Jason M. Hardy
89. *A Bonfire of Worlds* by Steven Mohan, Jr.
90. *Isle of the Blessed* by Steven Mohan, Jr.
91. *Embers of War* by Jason Schmetzer
92. *Betrayal of Ideals* by Blaine Lee Pardoe
93. *Forever Faithful* by Blaine Lee Pardoe
94. *Kell Hounds Ascendant* by Michael A. Stackpole
95. *Redemption Rift* by Jason Schmetzer
96. *Grey Watch Protocol (The Highlander Covenant, Book One)* by Michael J. Ciaravella
97. *Honor's Gauntlet* by Bryan Young
98. *Icons of War* by Craig A. Reed, Jr.
99. *Children of Kerensky* by Blaine Lee Pardoe
100. *Hour of the Wolf* by Blaine Lee Pardoe
101. *Fall From Glory (Founding of the Clans, Book One)* by Randall N. Bills
102. *Paid in Blood (The Highlander Covenant, Book Two)* by Michael J. Ciaravella
103. *Blood Will Tell* by Jason Schmetzer
104. *Hunting Season* by Philip A. Lee
105. *A Rock and a Hard Place* by William H. Keith, Jr.
106. *Visions of Rebirth* (Founding of the Clans, Book Two) by Randall N. Bills
107. *No Substitute for Victory* by Blaine Lee Pardoe
108. *Redemption Rites* by Jason Schmetzer
109. *Land of Dreams* (Founding of the Clans, Book Three) by Randall N. Bills
110. *A Question of Survival* by Bryan Young
111. *Jaguar's Leap* by Reed Bishop

YOUNG ADULT NOVELS

1. *The Nellus Academy Incident* by Jennifer Brozek
2. *Iron Dawn (Rogue Academy, Book 1)* by Jennifer Brozek
3. *Ghost Hour (Rogue Academy, Book 2)* by Jennifer Brozek
4. *Crimson Night (Rogue Academy, Book 3)* by Jennifer Brozek

OMNIBUSES

1. *The Gray Death Legion Trilogy* by William H. Keith, Jr.
2. *The Blood of Kerensky Trilogy* by Michael A. Stackpole

NOVELLAS/SHORT STORIES

1. *Lion's Roar* by Steven Mohan, Jr.
2. *Sniper* by Jason Schmetzer
3. *Eclipse* by Jason Schmetzer
4. *Hector* by Jason Schmetzer
5. *The Frost Advances (Operation Ice Storm, Part 1)* by Jason Schmetzer
6. *The Winds of Spring (Operation Ice Storm, Part 2)* by Jason Schmetzer
7. *Instrument of Destruction (Ghost Bear's Lament, Part 1)*
   by Steven Mohan, Jr.
8. *The Fading Call of Glory (Ghost Bear's Lament, Part 2)* by Steven Mohan, Jr.
9. *Vengeance* by Jason Schmetzer
10. *A Splinter of Hope* by Philip A. Lee
11. *The Anvil* by Blaine Lee Pardoe
12. *A Splinter of Hope/The Anvil* (omnibus)
13. *Not the Way the Smart Money Bets (Kell Hounds Ascendant #1)*
    by Michael A. Stackpole
14. *A Tiny Spot of Rebellion (Kell Hounds Ascendant #2)*
    by Michael A. Stackpole
15. *A Clever Bit of Fiction (Kell Hounds Ascendant #3)* by Michael A. Stackpole
16. *Break-Away (Proliferation Cycle #1)* by Ilsa J. Bick
17. *Prometheus Unbound (Proliferation Cycle #2)* by Herbert A. Beas II
18. *Nothing Ventured (Proliferation Cycle #3)* by Christoffer Trossen
19. *Fall Down Seven Times, Get Up Eight (Proliferation Cycle #4)* by Randall N. Bills
20. *A Dish Served Cold (Proliferation Cycle #5)*
    by Chris Hartford and Jason M. Hardy
21. *The Spider Dances (Proliferation Cycle #6)* by Jason Schmetzer
22. *Shell Games* by Jason Schmetzer
23. *Divided We Fall* by Blaine Lee Pardoe
24. *The Hunt for Jardine (Forgotten Worlds, Part One)* by Herbert A. Beas II
25. *Rock of the Republic* by Blaine Lee Pardoe
26. *Finding Jardine (Forgotten Worlds, Part Two)* by Herbert A. Beas II
27. *The Trickster (Proliferation Cycle #7)* by Blaine Lee Pardoe
28. *The Price of Duty* by Jason Schmetzer
29. *Elements of Treason: Duty* by Craig A. Reed, Jr.
30. *Mercenary's Honor* by Jason Schmetzer
31. *Elements of Treason: Opportunity* by Craig A. Reed, Jr.

ANTHOLOGIES

1. *The Corps (BattleCorps Anthology, Volume 1)* edited by Loren. L. Coleman
2. *First Strike (BattleCorps Anthology, Volume 2)* edited by Loren L. Coleman
3. *Weapons Free (BattleCorps Anthology, Volume 3)* edited by Jason Schmetzer
4. *Onslaught: Tales from the Clan Invasion* edited by Jason Schmetzer
5. *Edge of the Storm* by Jason Schmetzer
6. *Fire for Effect (BattleCorps Anthology, Volume 4)* edited by Jason Schmetzer
7. *Chaos Born (Chaos Irregulars, Book 1)* by Kevin Killiany
8. *Chaos Formed (Chaos Irregulars, Book 2)* by Kevin Killiany
9. *Counterattack (BattleCorps Anthology, Volume 5)* edited by Jason Schmetzer
10. *Front Lines (BattleCorps Anthology Volume 6)*
    edited by Jason Schmetzer and Philip A. Lee
11. *Legacy* edited by John Helfers and Philip A. Lee
12. *Kill Zone (BattleCorps Anthology Volume 7)* edited by Philip A. Lee
13. *Gray Markets (A BattleCorps Anthology),*
    edited by Jason Schmetzer and Philip A. Lee
14. *Slack Tide (A BattleCorps Anthology),*
    edited by Jason Schmetzer and Philip A. Lee
15. *The Battle of Tukayyid* edited by John Helfers
16. *The Mercenary Life* by Randall N. Bills
17. *The Proliferation Cycle* edited by John Helfers and Philip A. Lee
18. *No Greater Honor (The Complete Eridani Light Horse Chronicles)*
    edited by John Helfers and Philip A. Lee
19. *Marauder* by Lance Scarinci

MAGAZINES

1. *Shrapnel Issues #01–#09*

Made in the USA
Middletown, DE
20 December 2022